RACING INTO TROUBLE

Also by Maggie Dana

Keeping Secrets, Timber Ridge Riders
The Golden Horse of Willow Farm, Weekly Reader Books
Remember the Moonlight, Weekly Reader Books
Best Friends series, Troll Books

TIMBER RIDGE RIDERS
❧ Book Two ❧

RACING INTO TROUBLE

Maggie Dana

PAGEWORKS PRESS

ISBN 978-0-9851504-1-9

Edited by Judith Cardanha
Cover by Margaret Sunter
Interior design by Anne Honeywood
Published by Pageworks Press
Text set in Sabon

For Marina

1

KATE MCGREGOR'S HORSE HALTED, ears pricked on high alert. Blocking the road ahead was a red-and-gold moving van. Two men carried a huge white sofa up the loading ramp. Another followed, hefting a mattress wrapped in plastic that billowed in the wind.

Snap, crackle, flap.

Magician snorted and danced sideways.

"Easy boy," Kate said. "It's okay."

Kate's friend Holly Chapman skidded her wheelchair to a stop. "That's Denise's house," she said, pointing toward the yellow Cape. "Did you know the Elliotts were moving?"

"No, but I bet Angela's bummed."

"*Seriously* bummed," Holly said, with a fake groan. "She'll have nobody to hang out with any more."

Kate shuddered. Angela Dean was the only bad part about living at Timber Ridge, the posh community where Holly's mother, Liz, ran the riding school. Ever since Kate's arrival, Angela—egged on by Denise—had pulled one dirty trick after another. Kate tried to keep out of their way, but it was impossible. They were all on the riding team and practiced together every day, or they did whenever Angela and Denise bothered to show up.

Sweat trickled down Kate's cheeks. She yanked off her hard hat and ran a hand through her damp brown hair. She'd have liked to finish her ride without the helmet, but Liz was adamant about safety.

She plunked her helmet back on, left the strap dangling, and leaned forward to feel Magician's neck. They'd walked the last mile or so, and he was nicely cooled off. In a couple of minutes, they'd be back at the barn.

"Maybe your mother knows something we don't," Kate said.

"I doubt it. Mom's always the last to learn who's moving in and out around here," Holly said, "unless it's a horse, and then she knows about it before anyone else does."

"We'd better hurry up. She said to be back by six," Kate said. "She's going out, remember?"

"Yes, but where?" Holly said, wheeling herself forward. "Mom never goes out. She's always too tired. Last night she fell asleep over dinner."

Kate shrugged. "Maybe she's got a hot date."

"Mom?" Holly said. "You *have* to be joking."

Ever since Kate first met the Chapmans, she'd had a secret fantasy, one she hadn't even shared with Holly. Kate dreamed that she could get her widowed father and Holly's mom together. But her father's passion was butterflies, and Liz's was, well, horses. Kate could understand that.

As they maneuvered past the van, Kate glanced up at Timber Ridge Mountain. It wasn't the highest in Vermont, but it had some of the steepest ski trails in New England. A cable car snaked its way to the summit, taking summer visitors up for the magnificent view. When winter came, the cable car would be packed with brightly dressed skiers. There'd be Christmas lights and sleigh rides and ice skating on the pond.

By then, she'd be long gone from Timber Ridge. Her summer job as Holly's companion would be over in September, and if her father wasn't home from his Brazilian field trip, she'd have to move back in with her aunt. Aunt Marion was great, but her spare bed had more bumps than a bag full of apples.

"About time you two showed up," came a voice.

Kate pulled her scattered wits together as Liz Chapman emerged from the barn's indoor arena and strode toward them. With her deep blue eyes, friendly smile, and tousled blond hair, Liz looked young enough to be Holly's sister rather than her mother.

"The flies are bad today, so I've kept the horses inside," Liz said. "Don't forget to add vitamins to their grain, and only give Marmalade one flake of hay. He's getting too fat. And make sure the workmen haven't left any gates open."

"Workmen?" Holly said.

"They showed up an hour ago. Brought a load of lumber and supplies to repair the barn."

"Do we need to move the horses?" Kate said.

"Not yet. The roofers won't begin till next week," Liz said. "Leave the horses in their stalls, and turn the ponies outside." She pulled a tangle of keys from her pocket. "Did I forget anything?"

"Yes." Holly grinned. "Where are you going?"

"I'll be home by nine-thirty."

"Mom," Holly said. "Don't you *want* to tell us?"

Kate winked at her. "Maybe she *does* have a date."

"A date?" Liz said. "Who's got a date?"

"You," Holly said. Her blue eyes flashed with fun. "It's okay if you've got a secret admirer and you're too embarrassed to let on. We understand."

"Holly, I don't have a clue what you're talking about," Liz said. "And I don't have time to find out. I'm already late. Look, I'll see you kids later, okay?"

"Fine, fine," Holly said. "But suppose we need you?"

Liz held up her cell phone. "Call me."

"*If* you remember to turn it on," Holly said.

"Oops." Liz pressed a button, and the phone chimed into life. "I'll be at Larchwood, checking on a horse."

"You're buying another horse?" Kate said. That was exciting news—far more exciting than Liz having a date, though that would've been nice, too. The only horse the Chapmans owned was Holly's gelding, Magician. All the other horses at the stables were either owned by the residents of Timber Ridge or belonged to the stables as school horses.

"No," Liz said. "But—"

Her cell phone rang. She flipped it open, then frowned. "Yes, yes. I'm on my way."

"Mom?"

"I'll explain later," Liz said. "Just make sure the

horses don't starve, and help yourselves to whatever's in the fridge." She dropped a kiss on Holly's forehead. "I'd better get a move on. Mrs. Dean will be furious if I keep him waiting."

"Who?" Holly said.

"Giles Ballantine."

"Aha!" Holly gave Kate a thumbs-up. "You were right. Mom's got a hot date."

Liz shot her an exasperated look, jumped into the barn's truck, and took off amid a shower of gravel. Kate stared after her. Liz was wearing stained breeches, scuffed boots, and no hint of makeup. Not exactly date-worthy.

Kate slid off Magician, loosened his girth, and led him into the barn. "I wonder what's got your mom all steamed up."

"Mrs. Dean, probably," Holly said.

Magician sniffed her wheelchair, then nudged it with his nose. The chair didn't faze him one bit, not like flapping plastic or monster mattresses.

"Mrs. Dean's always in a lather about something," Kate said.

Holly pulled a face. "You don't suppose—"

"What?"

"The old witch set Mom up on a blind date?"

"Eewww," Kate said. "That's gross."

But the more she thought about it, the less ridiculous it seemed. Mrs. Dean had been trying to replace Liz for years. So far, nothing had worked because Liz did a bang-up job with the stables and the riding team was hugely successful. But if Liz met someone special and moved away from Timber Ridge, Mrs. Dean could force the homeowners' association to hire another barn manager, one who'd do exactly what she wanted—keep Angela on the team, no matter how badly she behaved or performed.

* * *

While Kate dished out the hay, Holly measured grain and vitamins into feed buckets, but she couldn't help turn the ponies out. Mom had forbidden her to lead a horse while she was in her wheelchair.

The list of things she could no longer do was endless, so Holly concentrated on the things she *could* do—like grooming the lower half of her horse, cleaning a bridle better than anyone else, and learning to ride all over again on Plug, the barn's beginner pony.

When Magician finished eating, Holly wheeled herself into his stall. He whickered softly and lowered his velvety nose so she could hug him. She rubbed his ears and ran her hands all over the parts of him she could reach—legs, shoulders, the underside of his belly. His coat was a rich, dark brown—so dark it was almost black . . . the color of a wet seal.

From the doorway, Kate said, "Angela's here."

"Did she come to help with barn chores?"

Kate grinned. "That'll be the day."

Holly gave Magician one last hug and joined Kate in the aisle. Toward them sauntered Angela Dean. Her white jeans fitted like a second skin, and her strappy sandals were just the sort of shoes you shouldn't be wearing in a barn full of horses. Her black hair, thick and glossy, was piled on top of her head and held in place by a tortoiseshell clip.

Ignoring them, Angela swept into the tack room. Moments later, she was back out again. "Where's my curling iron?"

"Your *what*?" Holly said.

"I left it here last night," Angela said, "in my grooming box."

"Curling Skywalker's mane, were you?" Kate said.

Angela glared at her. "Somebody's taken it."

"Not me." Holly tugged at her blond ponytail sticking out the back of her faded pink baseball cap. Angela had enviably straight hair. Why ruin it with stupid ringlets? "I don't need a curling iron, and neither do you."

"Says who?" Angela fixed her icy blue eyes on Kate. "Did *you* take it?"

"Nope."

"Well, it's gone," Angela said. "And it'd better show up fast, or—"

"You'll poke us with hair pins?" Holly burst into giggles. Last week Angela had accused Kate of stealing her curry comb, which was a joke, given that Angela barely ever bothered to groom her horse. It had turned up in Denise Elliott's tack trunk.

Kate said, "Is Denise moving out?"

"Yes," Angela said. "But what's it to you?"

"Nothing," Holly said. "Except you've just lost your best friend."

Angela shrugged. "Big deal. Denise was a drag, anyway."

"So who's moving in?" Holly said.

"Give me one good reason why I should tell you."

"Because you're dying to spill the beans."

Kate bent to whisper in Holly's ear. "Let's go home. We'll ask Liz when she gets back."

But Angela heard. "Oh, she's gone, then. Good thing,

too. My mother was afraid she'd be late." She pulled lip gloss from her pocket and smeared it across her mouth. The smell of coconut mingled with manure and fresh hay. "Mr. Ballantine's a very important man. He hates to be kept waiting."

Forcing herself to sound casual, Holly said, "Who is he?"

"An old friend of my father. He's buying one of Larchwood's best horses, and I'm going to ride it for him."

Kate said, "That's, like, twenty miles away."

"I'll be riding him here," Angela said. She yanked the clip out of her hair. It fell loose and framed her pale face like a shiny black curtain. "Buccaneer's a show jumper, and he'll make mincemeat out of our dumb little fences."

"Not so little," Holly said. "Some are over four feet."

"Kid's stuff," Angela said. "I've jumped them all."

"You flubbed the double oxer," Holly said, "even after Mom got on Skywalker and showed you how."

Angela shrugged. "So what!"

"Does Mr. Ballantine live at Timber Ridge?" Kate said.

"No, but then you wouldn't know that," Angela said. "You only *work* here."

Holly put a warning hand on Kate's arm. No point in

10

arguing, because Angela was right. Kate *did* work at the barn, but she'd also become Holly's best friend and a big part of Holly's small family. Just her and Mom . . . and now Kate.

"So, who's moving into the Elliotts' old house?" Holly said.

"Lord and Lady West," Angela said. "They're *English*."

For once Holly was speechless. *Lord?*

"And if you meet them," Angela went on, "you'll have to curtsy, so you'd better practice."

Holly looked at her legs, then at Angela. "Fat chance of that," she said, rolling her eyes. "Besides, we don't do lords and ladies in this country."

"We do now," Angela said. "And—"

"No way," Kate said. "It's in the Constitution."

"Ancient history." Angela flicked a wisp of hay off her spotless blue shirt. "Jennifer West is my very best friend."

"Best of the West," Holly muttered.

"She's flying in tonight, ahead of her parents, and she'll be staying with us until their house is ready," Angela said. "My mother went to school with Lady West, and my father—"

Kate said, "Does Jennifer ride?"

11

"Yes," Angela said. "And just wait till you see her. She's way better than you, Kate McGregor. Jennifer's grandmother was an Olympic rider, and her father trains dressage horses. He's got a breeding farm the size of—"

"Our back paddock?" Holly said.

Angela glared at her, then turned toward Kate. "You'll never get on the riding team now."

"Wrong," Holly said. "Kate will take Denise's place."

"Double wrong," Angela said. "The team only needs three riders. Me and Robin Shapiro"—there was a dramatic pause—"*and* Jennifer West."

"Wrong again," Holly said. "Mom always has four."

"In that case," Angela said, "she'll put Sue Piretti back on."

Holly felt herself blanch. She glanced up at Kate. Her mossy green eyes were wide open with shock. They'd forgotten all about Sue. She'd gotten hurt just before the Hampshire Classic, and Kate had taken her place at the last minute.

A younger kid poked her head around the barn door—Angela's little sister, Marcia.

"Hurry up," she said. "Mom's waiting."

Still staring at Kate and Holly, Angela flashed a dangerous smile. "Just don't forget. Jennifer West is *my* best friend, so you two had better keep away from her."

"No problem," Holly said. "She sounds like a pain."

"Angela," Marcia yelled, still at the door. "We found your curling iron."

"Where?" Holly said. Not that she cared, but it'd be nice to see Angela squirm.

Marcia's head disappeared.

With a toss of her hair, Angela flounced out of the barn without even stopping to pat her horse, a bay gelding that had cost Angela's parents a small fortune.

"Bratface," Holly said. "And I bet Jennifer is, too."

Kate grabbed a broom. "Brat or not," she said, sweeping vigorously, "if she's as good as Angela says, your mom will put her on the team."

"She won't."

"Mrs. Dean will insist."

"Don't worry," Holly said. "I bet Angela's just showing off, the way she always does." She rolled toward the barn door. "I'm hot enough to melt. Let's go jump in the pool."

Swimming was the one sport Holly excelled at.

2

NO MATTER WHAT STROKE Kate used, she was no match for Holly, who churned through the water like a torpedo.

"How about the dog paddle?" Holly said.

Kate hauled herself out of the pool. "You'd win that, too."

"Chicken," Holly said. She pushed off the edge and arched backward like a dolphin.

Or a mermaid, Kate thought. Brilliant in the water, but hopeless on land. There was nothing physical that prevented Holly from walking—no damage to her spine or her brain. Now and then, her toes would tingle and Holly would get her hopes up. At the Hampshire Classic, when Kate and the team won the challenge cup, it had slipped from Kate's grasp and landed on Holly's foot.

She'd felt it.

But the sensation faded, and now she was back to numb again. The doctors called it hysterical paralysis, caused by the car accident two years ago that had killed her father.

Holly refused to talk about it.

Kate didn't know how she stood it. Watching others ride had to be pure torture, knowing you could do it better with both hands tied behind your back. She'd once been a star rider, and her bedroom overflowed with the ribbons and trophies Holly had won at horse shows all over New England.

Holly surfaced. "I just thought of something."

"What?"

"Now that Denise is gone, Angela won't have anyone to help her play dirty tricks on you."

"Unless she recruits Jennifer West," Kate said.

* * *

Kate and Holly were sharing a roll of peppermint Life Savers when Liz staggered through the door at nine-thirty. She sank into a chair and pulled off her boots. "I'm starving. Is there anything left to eat?"

"Cold pizza," Kate said. "Can I get you some?"

"Yes, please," Liz said. "And a glass of seltzer."

15

Anxious not to miss anything, Kate hustled into the kitchen and whipped leftovers from the fridge. The seltzer she and Holly had opened earlier was flat, so she grabbed another bottle, plucked an apple from the fruit bowl, and raced back to the living room.

"Boy, that was fast," Liz said.

"Come on, Mom," Holly said. "Tell us what's going on. How was your date?"

"A complete waste of time. And it wasn't a date."

"We know. Angela told us about Mr. Ballantine." Holly tossed a mint into her mouth. "*And* the new family."

"But why was it a waste?" Kate asked.

"Because Giles Ballantine had already made up his mind to buy the horse, no matter what I said."

"He sounds like Mrs. Dean," Holly muttered.

Kate grinned. "Her evil twin brother."

"Buccaneer's got enormous potential," Liz said, through a mouthful of pepperoni pizza, "but he's high strung, and—"

"Skittish?" Holly said.

"More like willful," Liz said. "He needs a strong rider. Someone who knows what they're doing."

"Well, that let's Angela out," Kate said.

Liz frowned. "What do you mean?"

"She said that Buccaneer is coming here and that she's going to ride him."

"In her dreams," Liz said. "Even I'll have a tough time controlling him."

Kate found it hard to imagine Liz having a tough time with any horse. Last week, when Angela couldn't get Skywalker to jump the double oxer, Liz took over. She circled the fractious bay gelding at a slow trot, then a canter, and, in a few easy strides, faced him squarely at the difficult jump. They cleared it with ease.

"How big is he?" Holly said.

"What color?" added Kate.

"Sixteen hands and black as coal dust," Liz said. "He's got a star and two white socks."

"Which legs?" Kate said, anxious for every detail.

"Left side," Liz said. "He's fine boned, like a Thoroughbred, and he's got an amazingly long mane. His forelock reaches halfway down his nose." She paused for a sip of seltzer. "I wouldn't be surprised if he had a touch of Fresian blood as well."

"What about Mr. Ballantine?"

"No blood at all," Liz said, "as far as I could tell."

Holly laughed. "Be serious, Mom."

"He's tall and husky, with bushy eyebrows and a fierce-looking beard. He wears Levis and cowboy boots, and he's got a surprisingly soft voice."

"Does he ride Western?" Kate said.

"He doesn't ride at all."

"So why's he buying a horse?"

Liz shrugged. "Prestige, maybe? Celebrities buy unsuitable things all the time, especially horses."

"Is Mr. Ballantine a celebrity?"

"Kind of," Liz said. "He's a movie director."

"Why's he sending the horse to our barn? Why not leave him at Larchwood?" Holly said. "I mean, they've got a trainer, even if he's not nearly as good as you are."

"Mrs. Dean convinced him to send the horse here."

"Something else for her to show off about," Holly said. She gave an elaborate sigh. "We've got a *famous* horse at our barn. His owner makes *movies*, don't you know."

Kate giggled. "So, when's he coming?"

"Tomorrow afternoon," Liz said, with a yawn. "I'm ready for bed. I've got a busy day. The farrier's due at eight, I have lessons all morning, and the vet will be here after lunch for shots and worming. On top of all that, Mrs. Dean wants me to prepare a photo collage, and I've got two stalls to get ready.

"Two?" Holly said.

"One for Buccaneer and one for Jennifer West's horse. He's arriving this weekend."

* * *

"So, Mom did know about Jennifer," Holly said as she and Kate were getting ready for bed. "I wonder why she didn't tell us."

Kate shrugged. "Probably forgot."

"I bet she'll have a fancy accent," Holly said.

"And a snooty nose," Kate said, sticking hers in the air and flouncing around the room. She tripped over Holly's wooden rocking horse and landed in a heap of *Young Rider* magazines.

Holly said, "Her white stallion will wear a jeweled noseband."

"He'll have a sparkly saddle," Kate said.

"With silver stirrups."

"And she'll have a groom and two footmen."

"Like Cinderella."

Kate picked at a broken fingernail, then held it up for inspection. "Her hands will be too delicate for barn work, so—"

"—Princess Angela will order us to do it for her."

Despite her giggles, Kate knew it wasn't fair to judge

people without knowing them. But this new girl sounded awful, like she'd be just as bad as Angela. Maybe, even worse.

"It's kinda funny," Holly said, "but Angela's never said a word about Jennifer West before."

"She's been too busy tormenting me."

"Don't let her get to you."

Kate climbed into her pajamas. "I try, but—"

"Look," Holly said. "Mom's not going to drop you from the team, no matter how good this Jennifer is. Besides, we haven't seen her ride. I bet she's even worse than Angela."

But Kate wasn't so sure. It sounded as if Jennifer West had all the right credentials—an Olympic grandmother and a father who trained dressage horses. How could she be anything *but* a good rider?

* * *

Kate had just turned Plug and Snowball loose when Larchwood's red-and-black horse trailer pulled into the driveway. It rumbled toward her, swaying from side to side. She stepped back to let it pass.

A bellowing neigh erupted. Hooves clanged against metal.

Crash, bang, wallop.

Whatever was inside wanted desperately to get out.

Buccaneer!

Kate latched the paddock gate and ran after the trailer. Buccaneer neighed again and set off a chain reaction. Plug and Snowball, reluctant to move at the best of times, galloped across the paddock, tails flying, noses in the air. Marmalade, busy with a pile of hay, looked up, interested.

From the stables came a chorus of neighs.

The driver lowered his window. "Where to, Miss?"

"Wait here. I'll get Liz."

Kate sprinted into the barn and raced down the aisle. On both sides, horses paced their stalls, tense with excitement. Magician whickered; Skywalker banged at his door. Kate found Liz in her office with Holly, hunched over the laptop. Beside them was a box of photos. Old-time rock 'n' roll—Holly's favorite—blared from a radio perched on the shelf above Liz's messy desk.

"He's here," Kate gasped.

"The vet?"

"Buccaneer. Can't you hear him?"

Liz flicked off the radio and scrambled to her feet. "Kate, get a bucket of grain. Holly, make sure all the kids stay in the barn."

"They've gone home," Kate said. "Except for Marcia Dean."

"Where is she?" Liz grabbed her gloves and made for the door.

"Outside, waiting for her mother."

"Keep her out of the way."

And Liz was gone.

"What a lot of fuss," Holly said, as Kate pushed her outside. "Surely this horse can't be *that* bad."

* * *

Nostrils flaring, Buccaneer exploded down the ramp. He snorted and pawed at the ground. Holly couldn't take her eyes off him; any minute now, he'd be breathing fire. Sweat covered his neck and shoulders, thick and frothy like whipped egg white. Gobs of foam flew from his mouth.

"Stand back," Liz yelled.

She gripped Buccaneer's lead rope in both hands. With steady words and a gentle voice, she tried to calm him. But the black gelding wasn't having any of it. He squealed and kicked out. One of his leg bandages flapped loose.

"Easy boy, easy," Liz said as Buccaneer danced in a

circle around her. She waved at Kate. "Give me the grain."

Kate passed her the bucket. Liz shook it gently. The horse stopped whirling for a second or two. Breathing hard, he eyed the bucket, then made a tiny step forward and stuck out his nose.

"That's right," Liz said, edging closer. "I won't hurt you."

With another snort, Buccaneer plunged his nose into the bucket and scattered grain in all directions. Liz waited a few seconds, then laid her hand on his cheek. Holly's breath came out in a whoosh. No matter how many times she watched her mother gentle a difficult horse, it was always scary.

A boy with floppy blond hair climbed out of the truck's cab. He folded his arms and leaned against its shiny red fender. Holly caught his eye.

She nudged Kate. "That's Adam Randolph."

"Who?" Kate held up a hand to shade her eyes.

"We met him at the show, remember?" Holly said. "He's on the Larchwood team and rides that flashy Arabian pinto. They won the silver medal."

Kate shrugged.

"You are *so* fake," Holly said, grinning.

They'd talked about him for hours and laughed at the way Angela had thrown herself at him. Adam barely noticed, and when she invited him to a fancy barbecue at her parents' hotel, he said he wasn't hungry. But the minute Angela stormed off, he sneaked fries from Holly's plate and finished off Kate's hot dog, then ordered more.

"Want help?" Adam said to Liz. "I know this horse."

"Great," Liz replied. "See if you can get that loose bandage."

"Sure, no problem."

Smoothly, he unwrapped it and took off the others as well. Buccaneer, still busy with his bucket, paid no attention. Adam wadded up the bandages and dumped them in the truck, then ambled toward Kate and Holly, hands in his pockets and whistling off-key.

Kate stared at her feet.

Holly knew exactly what she was thinking . . . same as she was. *Why did he have to show up now, of all times, when they were hot and sweaty and wearing their rattiest barn clothes?*

"Hey," Adam said. "It was my fault—about the bandages." He shifted from one foot to the other. "I do a lousy job of wrapping. I'd make a terrible nurse."

"You could've gotten your head kicked in," Holly said.

He grinned. "Buc's not a mean horse. He just spooks easy."

There was a whirl of dust, and Mrs. Dean's silver Mercedes cruised down the driveway. She parked crookedly beside the Larchwood trailer and rolled down her window.

"Hurry up, Marcia. We're late for tennis."

Marcia streaked across the gravel and leaped into the front seat. The car backed up a couple of feet, then stopped. Its rear doors opened, and Angela climbed out— followed by a girl Holly didn't recognize.

3

ANGELA DROPPED HER TENNIS RACQUET and rushed toward Buccaneer. He whipped his nose from the bucket. Wild-eyed, he looked from Angela to Liz and then reared, almost pulling Liz off her feet.

Kate yanked Holly's wheelchair out of the way so fast that Holly almost fell out. Adam grabbed Angela and shoved her against the Mercedes. The other girl—it had to be Jennifer—raced down the driveway and closed the main gate.

Buccaneer reared again, ears pinned, legs thrashing. Liz ducked, and his flailing hooves missed her by inches.

"Mom," Holly yelled. "Let him go."

"She can't," Kate said. "He'll get tangled in the rope."

"He's freaking out," Holly wailed. "Somebody, *do* something." She slapped her knees. "If I could walk, I'd—"

"Liz knows what she's doing," Kate said, watching her inch closer to the horse—hand over hand along Buccaneer's lead rope. Good thing she was wearing gloves. If he jerked away now, the rope would rip her hands to shreds.

"Easy, big fella. It's okay," Liz said.

Sides heaving, Buccaneer snorted and lowered his head. One ear came forward, then the other, back and forth, swiveling like antennae.

"Get those ponies out of the paddock," Liz said.

"Where to, Ma'am?" said the Larchwood driver.

"Turn them loose in the indoor arena, and leave the paddock gate open."

Adam and the Larchwood driver caught Plug and Snowball. The new girl followed with Marmalade, still munching wisps of hay. Kate shot them a grateful look. No way could she leave Holly. If Buccaneer erupted again, she'd never get herself to safety in time.

"Stupid, stupid Angela," Holly muttered. "I could kick her."

"No, you couldn't," Kate said. "But I'd do it for you."

"Where is she, anyway?" Holly looked around.

"In the car."

"Coward," Holly said. "She's scared Mom'll give her a tongue lashing."

"No time for that," Kate said. "She's got her hands full."

"Hold the gate for me," Liz yelled. "We're coming through."

Sensing freedom, Buccaneer bolted forward. Liz scrambled to keep up, and they barreled into the paddock like two puppets on the same strings. Kate swung the gate closed. After a few more skirmishes, Liz released Buccaneer's halter, and he spiraled into a tornado of bone-shattering bucks—one after another till he reached the far side.

He whirled and trotted back, almost in slow motion, feet barely seeming to touch the ground. With his arched neck and flagged tail, he reminded Kate of a wild stallion guarding his mares.

Buccaneer slid to a stop. He gave a great, bellowing neigh and got answers from half the barn.

"Way to go," Liz said. "Let 'em know you're here."

"Everything all right, Ma'am?" said the Larchwood driver.

"Yes, and thanks," Liz said.

The driver tipped his hat. "Then we'll be off."

Kate glanced toward the truck. Adam was unloading a ton of equipment—blankets, lead ropes, buckets, and a red tack trunk with gold initials on its side. Still whistling, he rolled up the messy bandages and added them to the pile. There was no sign of Jennifer West—or of Mrs. Dean's silver Mercedes.

Holly tugged at Kate's arm. "Go and say goodbye to Adam."

Kate kicked a clump of grass.

"Hurry up. They're leaving."

But the truck had already pulled away, and the last Kate saw of Adam was his freckled arm, waving through the side window.

"He's cute," Holly said.

"I guess."

Holly's cell phone buzzed. She flipped it open, grinned, and shoved it under Kate's nose. Adam had texted:

GR8 2 C U

"Sweet," Holly said. A blush crept up her face.

Kate felt herself blushing as well and turned away. Horses were a whole lot easier to deal with than boys.

They didn't write in nerdy code that took longer to read than proper words.

Straddling the paddock fence, Kate watched Buccaneer strut his stuff. His rock star attitude had caught her imagination, and she fantasized about being the only one besides Liz who'd be able to ride him. Angela certainly wasn't up to it, not by a long shot. She only won blue ribbons because her parents had bought her a push-button horse.

"So, what did you think of her?" Holly said.

Kate looked down. "Who?"

"Lady Jennifer."

"She closed the front gate and took Marmalade inside."

"Didn't you notice *anything*?" Holly said. "What about her spiked hair, the hoop earrings? They were big enough for parrots to perch in."

"So?"

Holly sighed. "She looks *nothing* like a rider."

* * *

The next morning, Kate was mucking out Magician's stall when Angela and Jennifer showed up. They wore spotless breeches and high boots and matching green t-shirts with *Timber Ridge* printed on the pocket. Kate

stared at them. Jennifer's horse wasn't due till the weekend, so who was she planning to ride?

"Where's Liz?" Angela said.

"In her office, I think."

"Jen's going to ride Skywalker, and I'll ride Buccaneer."

Kate propped her pitchfork against the wall. "You
can't."

"Why not?" Angela's eyes glinted.

"Because he hasn't settled in yet, and—"

There were half-a-dozen reasons why Angela couldn't
ride Buccaneer—he was too willful, she wasn't good
enough, Liz hadn't yet ridden him herself—but Kate
wasn't about to get into a shouting match over it.

"That's stupid," Angela said. "Of course, he's settled
in." She turned and stalked back down the aisle.

Magician, standing in the cross-ties, gave a loud
snort.

"Is that your horse?" Jennifer said.

She wasn't a bit like Holly described—no sign of
hoop earrings or spiked hair. Just a girl with hazel eyes,
reddish-brown curls, and a scatter of freckles. Maybe she
had two looks—one for the barn and another for everything else.

"No. He belongs to Holly," Kate said.

31

"Who's she?"

Hadn't Angela told her anything? "Liz's daughter."

"That girl in the wheelchair?"

"Yes."

"What's wrong with her?"

"She can't walk."

"I already figured that," Jennifer said. "But why?"

"Hysterical paralysis," Kate blurted, then could've kicked herself. It was none of Jennifer's business. But the girl's blunt question had caught her off guard. Were the English always this nosy?

"Then it's all in her head, right?"

Kate grabbed her pitchfork. She'd said enough already.

A door banged open and Liz emerged from her office. Angela, looking flushed and sulky, trailed behind. Liz had probably bawled her out for spooking Buccaneer.

"No, Angela, you can't ride him," Liz said. "And that's final."

"But Mr. Ballantine said I could."

With enormous patience, Liz said, "I can't risk it. Buccaneer's not suitable for you—or any of the kids—to ride." She laid both hands on Angela's shoulders. "I'm sorry, but that's just the way it is."

"Are *you* going to ride him?"

"Of course, I am," Liz said. "Mr. Ballantine sent him here for training." She glanced toward Kate and Jennifer. "Did you hear what I said, girls? Buccaneer's off limits."

Kate swallowed hard. There was no way Liz would let her ride Buccaneer now. And all because of Angela. Trust her to mess things up for the rest of them.

"Come on Jen," Angela said. "Let's get out of here."

"Why?"

"Because we've only got one horse, and—"

"We could take turns."

"Forget it," Angela snapped. "We'll play tennis instead." She gave Liz a pointed look. "I have a dozen racquets, so we won't have to share."

"Sure," Jennifer said. "Whatever."

There was a clatter of wheels, and Holly rolled out of the tack room. She'd been cleaning bridles and had saddle soap smeared up both arms. A blob of metal polish decorated her nose.

"Hey, Mom. You promised I could ride this morning."

Liz slapped her forehead. "Oh, sorry, I forgot." She looked at Kate. "Would you saddle up Plug, but give me another ten minutes, okay? I've got a couple of calls to make." She turned and ran back into her office.

Jennifer stared at Holly's legs. "You can *ride*?"

"Oh, puh-leeze," Angela said. "Let's get moving."

"No, wait," Jennifer said. "I'd like to watch."

"Don't bother," Angela said. "It's way beyond boring. All she does is plod around the ring on a scruffy little pony." She linked her arm through Jennifer's and dragged her down the aisle. "There's nothing for us to do here. We'll have more fun at the club."

When they reached the door, Jennifer hung back. She let Angela go ahead of her, then turned around and waved. "Nice to meet you."

Well, Kate thought. *Maybe she wasn't so bad after all.*

* * *

Holly didn't want to ride Plug. She begged for Magician, the way she always did. Ever since her first therapeutic riding lesson, she'd had one goal in mind: to get back on her own horse.

"I'll be fine, Mom. I know I will. He'll take care of me."

"Magician needs a strong pair of legs, Holly," her mother said. "You ought to know that."

"But—"

"No arguments," Liz said. "It's Plug or nothing. He's

steady as a rock, and if you fall off, he's a lot closer to the ground than Magician."

"Mom, it's like riding a toy bulldozer."

"That's perfect," Liz said. "Couldn't be better."

Holly rolled her eyes.

But her mother wouldn't budge, so Holly had to be content with Plug, the sturdy brown pony she'd learned to ride on when she was five. He was sweet and fuzzy and had adorable ears, but riding him wasn't the same as beating up the cross-country course on Magician or jumping against the clock.

The worst part was getting on Plug's back. Mom and Kate had to hoist her up while someone else stood at his head. Today, Robin pitched in, and they'd just gotten Holly upright when Plug rearranged his feet and stood on one of hers. With a startled cry, Holly fell sideways into her mother's arms.

Kate leaned against the pony's shoulder. "You clumsy beast."

"Stop," Holly said. "Don't move him."

"He's on your foot," Liz said, leaning into the pony as well.

"I know," Holly said. "I can *feel* him."

Liz stared at her. "What did you say?"

"Mom, it hurts. It really hurts."

With another mighty shove, Liz dislodged the pony's hoof. "Are you sure? I mean, we've been through this before."

"I know, Mom. I *know*. But this time it's real."

Holly slumped into her wheelchair. She knew all about people with no feet who suddenly felt their toes twitching. But this wasn't like that. She'd felt Plug's hoof—the way she'd felt the team's challenge cup when it landed on her foot two weeks ago.

They'd all whooped with delight.

Gently, Liz took off Holly's boot and moved her foot from side to side. "Can you feel that?"

"No."

"How about this?" Liz pressed her fingers against Holly's ankle, and then up toward her knee.

"Yes. No. Oh, I don't know," Holly wailed. "But honestly, Mom, I felt Plug's hoof. I *know* I did." She wanted to feel something—anything—so desperately, she was even tempted to fake it.

"Let's check with your doctor," Liz said. She whipped out her cell and punched in a number. "Maybe she can fit us in this afternoon."

Holly looked up at her mother, then up at Kate and

Robin. It was always up. Up, up, and forever *up* . . . never down.

Her view of the people around her was confined to their nostrils, the underside of their chins. She knew more about their knees and feet than she did about the tops of their heads. But that was going to change, starting right now.

"I'm going to walk again," she said. "You'll see."

It wasn't a false alarm. Not this time.

4

KATE STAYED BEHIND while Liz took Holly to the doctor. She kept glancing at the clock. Surely they'd be home soon. It had been, what, three hours since they left?

At six-thirty, the screen door slid open.

Holly wheeled herself inside, a pair of steel crutches balanced across her lap.

"Wow," Kate said, jumping up. "This is wicked cool."

"They're not for me." Holly's voice was flat.

"What happened?"

"Mom fell off the curb and sprained her ankle."

"That stinks," Kate said.

"Tell me about it," Holly said, whipping off her baseball cap. She shook out her ponytail and crammed the hat on backward.

"Is she okay?"

"Yeah," Holly said. "It's just slowed her down a bit."

"But what about you? Didn't the doctor say anything?"

"Same old stuff. Blah, blah, blah."

"Bummer," Kate said. "I'm so sorry." She wanted to say more, but that was taboo. Holly hated sympathy. If you even hinted life was unfair, she'd deny it and change the subject.

There was a noise outside. Kate leaned across Holly's wheelchair and saw Liz hobbling up the ramp. Clamped beneath one arm, she carried a riding boot. Kate slid the door open and Liz limped inside.

"Thanks," Liz said, collapsing on the couch. She propped her injured foot on the coffee table. Magazines and books slid off. Kate's empty glass tumbled onto the floor.

Kate stared at Liz's cast. It had buckles and Velcro straps, kind of like a ski boot, only not quite as big. "It's not broken is it?"

"Just a bad sprain," Liz said. "But I'll be out of action for a week or so." She shifted her foot and winced. "I'm going to need help, Kate. I'll cancel lessons, except for the beginners, but the horses have to be fed and cared for."

"No problem," Kate said. "I can handle the chores."

"Get the others to pitch in," Liz said. "*All* of them, including Angela."

Holly snorted. "When's the last time Angela helped anyone?"

"What about Buccaneer?" Kate said.

Liz groaned. "I'd forgotten about him," she said. "Well, he'll just have to wait till I'm back on my feet. Let's hope Mr. Ballantine's not in too much of a hurry to get his horse polished and ready to go."

"Then let Angela ride him," Holly said.

"No way," Liz said. "You saw what that horse is like."

"Only kidding, Mom."

Kate said, "I could ride him for you."

"I know," Liz said. "But not this time, Kate. I can't risk it. If you had an accident, I'd really be up the creek. Who'd do all the barn chores if you wound up on crutches as well?"

"And who'd feed us?" Holly said. "I'm starving."

* * *

After dinner, Kate and Holly loaded the dishwasher while Liz scribbled out a list of chores. She went over it with

Kate, crossed out a couple of items, then added three more.

"There," she finally said. "I think we've got it all covered."

Holly glanced at it. "Except for me."

"What do you mean?"

Holly held up a sheet of paper covered with diagrams. "Who's going to help me with these if Kate's at the barn all day?"

"I'm sorry, sweetie, but they'll just have to wait"

"They can't," Holly said.

"Honey," Liz said. "These new exercises don't guarantee anything."

"What exercises?" Kate said.

"She got them at the clinic," Liz said wearily. "She's convinced they'll get her walking again."

"Will they?"

"Maybe—maybe not," Liz said. "But you know Holly. A cross between a mule and an elephant—stubborn, with a long memory."

Holly stuck out her bottom lip. A tear rolled down one cheek, then another, and Kate realized it was the first time she'd ever seen Holly cry.

"I'll help," she said.

But how would she get it all done? Between barn chores, playing physical therapist, and making sure Liz and Holly didn't starve, she'd have time for nothing else.

Not even Buccaneer.

* * *

Pounding rain kept them awake half the night, and Holly refused to get out of bed.

"What's the point? I can't go outside. My wheels will get stuck in the mud." She turned over and went back to sleep . . . or pretended to.

Kate scrambled into her barn clothes, unearthed a yellow slicker from Holly's closet, and found Liz in the kitchen, wobbling about on her crutches and threatening to toss them out.

"I can't walk on these stupid things."

"Should I teach the beginners?" Kate said.

"Thanks, but I'll manage. You've got enough on your hands." Liz sank into a chair. "Where's Holly?"

"In a funk."

Liz sighed. "Then I'd better go and cheer her up."

Kate dumped cereal into her bowl and wolfed it down. She had two hours to feed horses, muck stalls, and clean up muddy ponies before lessons began at nine. On her way out the door, she grabbed another pack of Life Savers and stuffed it into her pocket. Who knew when she'd get lunch.

* * *

Horses whinnied and banged at their doors as Kate rushed about, measuring out grain and making sure everyone got enough hay. In the far stall, Buccaneer paced back and forth. His end of the barn was getting the worst of the storm. Rain dripped from rafters; wind rattled loose shingles and sent whirls of wood shavings spiraling down the aisle.

"Hang in there, boy," Kate said.

He flicked his ears and eyed her warily. She'd ask Liz about moving him elsewhere once the renovations began. Maybe he'd be better off in the paddock's run-in shed with Marmalade or Plug for company.

Kate was tacking up the last pony when the lesson kids began to arrive. In no time, the barn was pandemonium.

"But I want to ride Snowball. Liz *promised* I could."

"You can't. It's *my* turn."

"Marmalade's too slow. He won't even trot."

"Do I *have* to ride Plug?"

"Marcia, that's *my* helmet. Yours is over there."

Bit by bit, Kate sorted out the details of which kid got what horse, then herded them toward the indoor arena. Once they were safely inside, she ducked into the observation room and grabbed a folding chair for Liz.

"You think of everything," Liz said, sinking into it.

"Shall I stick around and help?"

"Thanks, but I'll be fine."

Kate hurried back to the stables. As she passed Buccaneer's stall, he stopped pacing and looked at her with curiosity. A hunk of forelock drooped over one eye. His mane, thick and wavy, hung to his shoulders. He took a step forward, then another. So did she. He was like a magnet, drawing her closer.

"Hey, big fella," Kate said.

He stuck his nose over the door. She held up her hand for him to sniff. He gave a little snort and his breath tickled her palm. Encouraged, Kate fumbled in her pocket for a carrot, but all she found were Life Savers. She opened the pack and popped one in her mouth. Buccaneer whickered.

Did horses like peppermint?

She offered him two. He whuffled them up like a vacuum cleaner and looked for more. Kate glanced down the aisle. No sign of anyone else. Liz would be tied up for another twenty minutes. She unlatched the stall door, then had second thoughts.

Maybe this was a really dumb idea. What if Buccaneer freaked out? Suppose she got caught breaking the rules? Liz had made it quite clear this horse was off-limits. But if Kate was going to make friends with Buccaneer, now was the time. She slid back the door and stepped inside.

* * *

For a few tense moments, they eyed one another. Kate stood perfectly still, hardly daring to breathe. *Let Buccaneer make the first move*, she thought. Sooner or later, he'd get curious enough to make contact. Buccaneer tossed his head and snorted; he stamped his foot.

"Come along, boy," Kate whispered. "I won't hurt you."

With another shake of his head, he leaned toward her, neck stretched as far as it would go, and nuzzled her pocket. The smell of mint wafted out. Buccaneer grunted, curled his upper lip, and showed Kate a fine set of teeth.

It looked as if he was laughing.

Kate let out her breath, unaware she'd been holding

it. She fed him another mint and stroked his glossy neck. Slowly, she ran her hands down his well-muscled shoulders. He didn't seem to mind, and she was about to massage his withers when a voice at the door stopped her cold.

"You'd better not let Mom see this."

Kate stared at her. "What are you doing here?"

"I could say the same about you." Holly's wheelchair was spattered with mud, her jeans soaking wet. She shook her ponytail vigorously and raindrops flew out.

Faint with relief, Kate patted Buccaneer and slipped him another mint. There were only four left.

"So, how did you tame the dragon?" Holly said.

"These"—Kate held up the Life Savers—"and my charming personality."

"Cool," Holly said. "We'll have to buy a case of them."

Behind her, the door from the indoor arena opened. Hooves clattered on concrete. Kids' voices rang out, and Liz yelled at someone to slow down.

"Uh, oh," Holly said. "You'd better hide."

"Where?"

"In the hayrack?"

"That's crazy," Kate whispered.

"Then climb out the window. I'll stall Mom as long as I can."

Liz's uneven footsteps—*clump, shuffle, clump*—drew closer. Kate steeled herself for the worst.

"What's going on here?" Liz said.

Holly swiveled her chair and blocked the doorway. "Mom, don't be mad," she said. "Kate's got him eating out of her hand. Look."

Maybe it was some sort of equine showmanship, or maybe it was just dumb luck, but Buccaneer chose that moment to rest his handsome head on Kate's shoulder. For added effect, he whickered softly and gobbled up another mint.

"Well, I'll be—" Liz scratched her head.

Kate took the plunge. "Let me ride him, please."

"You've *got* to, Mom," Holly said. "You can't ride for a week, and by then he'll explode."

Frowning, Liz looked from Kate to the horse and back again.

"I'll be careful," Kate said. "I promise." She wrapped her arms around Buccaneer's neck, and he closed his eyes.

"See," Holly said. "He's quieter than Marmalade."

Her mother pinned Kate with a look. "I'm not happy about this. But now that it's happened, we may as well take advantage. However, if Buccaneer gives one speck of trouble, I want you off his back immediately. Understood?"

Holly punched the air with her fist. "Wowee!"

"Should I lunge him first?" Kate said.

"He's better under saddle," Liz said. "I'll see you in the arena at noon. That'll give you enough time to help the kids and get yourself ready." Balanced awkwardly, she turned. "I'll be in my office."

"With your feet up?" Holly said.

Liz gave her a withering look and clumped off.

Not quite the reaction Kate had hoped for. "She wasn't exactly thrilled, was she?"

"She'll be fine about it," Holly said. "You'll see."

* * *

In a flurry of nervous excitement, Kate curried, brushed, and polished. She picked out Buccaneer's hooves and untangled his mane, then stood back to admire her handiwork.

"I've been thinking," Holly said.

"About how great he looks?"

"No, about you."

Kate rubbed her face with a cloth. "I'm a mess."

"You're also stuck between a rock and a hard place."

"I am?" Kate said, looking around. "How?"

"Think about it," Holly said. "On the one hand, make Buccaneer look easy to handle, and Angela will bug Mom about riding him . . . or Mrs. Dean will, and Mom will have to give in. On the other hand, if you flub it up, then—"

"I get the picture," Kate said, saddling Buccaneer. "I'm cooked either way."

"Yup."

"Now what?"

"Do an epic job and hope Angela never finds out."

"But suppose she shows up?" Kate said.

"She won't," Holly said. "It's Thursday, which means junior tennis at the club. She's in the semi-finals."

5

SIZZLING WITH ENERGY, Buccaneer bounced into the arena. Kate kept him in check, but only just. He responded to the lightest touch. All it took was a whisper of Kate's leg, a mere suggestion of her hands, and he was ready for action.

To keep him focused, Kate circled at a working trot in both directions and extended across the diagonal. Buccaneer's ground-covering stride gobbled up the tanbark. Maybe he'd been a dressage horse in another life or perhaps a show jumper. And who knew what his next role would be? With a movie director owner, he might even become a film star.

"Let's have a canter," Liz called out.

Kate gave the signal, and Buccaneer changed gears

without missing a beat. It was like riding a rocking horse.

Holly stuck up her thumbs. "Nice."

Sitting deep in the saddle, Kate guided him into a figure eight, and he performed a flawless flying change in the center. Even Magician couldn't do that. She tried it again from the other direction, and again he changed lead without being asked.

Another thumbs-up from Holly.

"Time for a break," Liz said. "Bring him over here."

Kate slowed to a walk. She kicked her feet free of the stirrups and headed for Liz, knowing she'd done well. Maybe a little *too* well. From what Liz said about *her* ride on Buccaneer, he hadn't performed like this for her. She'd either caught him on a bad day, or else it was the candy.

"Epic," Holly said.

Kate grinned. "Blame the Life Savers."

"*Life Savers?*" Liz said.

"Kate bribed him with peppermints," Holly said, laughing. "Smell his breath."

Liz's cell phone interrupted. Leaning on one crutch, she patted every pocket and seemed about to give up when Holly handed her the phone.

"You gave it to me, remember?" she said.

"Hello?" Liz said, as if surprised to get a call. Then, "Yes, of course, I still want it." She rolled her eyes. "All right, I'll meet you out back."

"Problem?" Kate said.

"Hay delivery," Liz said, pocketing her phone. "The driver's new and doesn't know where to unload."

She tucked the other crutch beneath her arm and winced. These newer ones, Kate knew, were supposed to be more comfortable than the old-fashioned wooden ones, but you'd never know that from looking at Liz's face. It was pinched and gray with pain. No wonder she was grumpy.

"Do you need help?" Kate said.

"No. Stay here and work on those circles," Liz said. "Use more leg to get him to bend. He's a little stiff in the corners."

That's all? Not, *Well done* or *That was terrific*?

Biting down hard on disappointment, Kate glanced at the jumps. Buccaneer's cooler was still draped over one of the side wings, where she'd left it to dry.

Liz shook her head. "Out of the question."

"How about the cross-rail, then?" Kate knew she was pushing her luck, but she really wanted to jump Buccaneer. He was a coiled spring, ready to leap out of his skin.

"Just the cavalettis."

Those weren't jumps. They were poles on the ground to help horses engage their hindquarters and improve their balance. Kate shoved her feet in the stirrups. Back to boring old circles. Maybe she'd vary the routine with half-halts or a shoulder-in. She waited for Liz to leave, then adjusted her helmet.

Holly leaned forward. "You guys looked great out there."

"Your mom didn't think so."

"She did," Holly said. "It's just that—"

"What?"

"Mom's under pressure again," Holly said. "Mrs. Dean's been bugging her to let Angela ride Buccaneer."

Kate snorted. "He's not exactly push-button."

"You could've fooled me," Holly said.

"Well, he's not," Kate said. "He's eager to please and he listens, but if you push the wrong button, he'll explode."

"Try telling Mrs. Dean that," Holly said. "She's also bugging Mom about that stupid photo collage."

"Can't anyone else do it?" Kate said. "Why dump it on Liz?"

"Because it's all about the riding team. Mrs. Dean wants to display it at the club in time for the Wests' arrival."

"Why?"

"Because Jennifer's Olympic grandmother is the centerpiece."

Kate looped the reins over one arm and fastened her chinstrap. "That's stretching it. I mean she never rode for Timber Ridge, did she?"

"No, but her granddaughter probably will."

"Has Liz—?" Kate faltered. They'd gone over this six ways from Sunday, worrying about who'd make the next team. Liz had more than enough qualified riders to choose from.

"Mom hasn't said a word," Holly said. "She's waiting for Jennifer's horse to get here."

Buccaneer snorted and stamped his foot.

"You'd better fix his girth," Holly said. "It looks kinda loose."

Kate flipped up her leg and saddle flap and was about to tighten the billets, when Buccaneer scuttled sideways like a crab. Taken by surprise, Kate lost her balance, and it was several heart-pounding moments before she righted herself. Next thing she knew, they were heading straight for the parallel bars.

"Pull away," Holly yelled.

But if she swerved now, they'd crash into the wings.

So Kate gave Buccaneer his head, and he cleared the red-and-white poles with inches to spare. Two strides later, he flew over the double oxer. His green cooler flapped in the breeze made by his legs.

Wow!

Kate wanted to do it again. So, obviously, did Buccaneer. He tossed his head and fought the bit. Flecks of foam spattered his neck and shoulders. But common sense got the better of Kate, so she circled him twice and trotted back to Holly.

"Awesome," Holly said. "Good thing Mom missed it."

Kate gulped. "Don't tell her."

"As if I would," Holly said, sounding indignant. "But you'd better cool him off before we go back. He's all sweaty."

After five minutes of jogging, Kate slowed to a walk and let Buccaneer have a loose rein. He stretched out his neck, and Kate allowed her mind to drift. She imagined riding Buccaneer on the trails that fanned up Timber Ridge Mountain like green fingers. They'd jump the cross-country course and explore the woods. She'd take him swimming at the lake and—

There was a shout, and her reverie was broken by the

sound of Holly arguing with the last person Kate wanted to see.

* * *

Reluctantly, Kate rode toward them. Why was Angela here with Jennifer and not at the club? Neither was dressed for riding. Angela wore jeggings and a crop top; Jennifer slouched against the rail in checkerboard sneakers and a gray hoodie that reached to her knees. Outside, wind and rain lashed the arena's cavernous roof. Of course! How could she have been so dumb? They couldn't play tennis in this weather.

Holly's voice rose above the storm. "No way will Mom let you ride Buccaneer." She swiveled toward Kate. "Don't listen to Angela. She's lying."

"Am not," Angela retorted. "My mother just cleared it with Liz. If you don't believe me, ask Jen."

Holly rounded on Jennifer. "Did she?"

Jennifer shrugged. "I guess so."

She sounded more American than British. Maybe Angela had made it all up, about Jennifer's parents being Lord and Lady West. It'd be just like Angela to tell whopping stories to make herself look important.

Angela reached for Buccaneer's reins. He flattened his ears and jerked away.

"Careful," Kate said, bringing him back. "He's spooky."

"But you handle him beautifully," Angela said, with a sly smile. "Liz is so impressed that she says it's okay for me to ride him as well."

Stunned into silence, Kate could only stare. She'd never seen Angela smile before. It was like watching a hyena bare its teeth. She glanced at Holly, who clutched her throat and made gagging noises.

Angela put a hand on Kate's stirrup. "Get off. It's my turn."

"I'd rather wait till Liz gets back," Kate said.

There was a dangerous pause. Then Angela said, "Jen and I were in the observation room. We saw you take the parallel bars *and* the oxer." She narrowed her eyes. "Did Liz give you permission to jump?"

In a flash, Kate saw where Angela was going with this. Let her ride Buccaneer, and she wouldn't say a word about Kate's unauthorized jump. Refuse, and she'd blab it all over the barn. It was just another of Angela's dirty little tricks—blackmail dressed up in fake smiles and false flattery, and there was nothing Kate could do about it.

Desperately, she looked at Holly. "Um—"

Holly shook her head so violently, her baseball cap flew off and landed well beyond her reach. Without thinking, Kate dismounted and scooped up the cap. It had *Boss Mare* embroidered across the front. She brushed off the flecks of tanbark.

"Quick, behind you," Holly warned.

Kate whirled around, but too late. Angela had her foot in the empty stirrup and was swinging herself awkwardly over Buccaneer's back. She landed in the saddle with a thump. The nervous horse leaped forward like a startled rabbit.

"Angela, come back," Kate cried. "You'll get hurt."

Buccaneer took off. Angela's hair whipped loose from its clip and streamed behind her. No helmet, no body protector. She wasn't even wearing riding boots. In mounting horror, Kate watched Angela tug at Buccaneer's mouth, sawing from side to side. He wore a jointed snaffle—mild in the right hands, but horrible in the wrong ones.

Down the arena they tore, scattering tanbark in all directions. Buccaneer skidded to a stop, then careened madly around the corner, almost scraping his rider off against the rails.

Jennifer tugged at Kate's arm. "Stop her."

"How?" Kate said. "Throw myself in front of them?"

"Don't be stupid," Holly said. "Get out the Life Savers."

Kate fumbled in her pocket as Buccaneer galloped back toward them. Stirrups flying, Angela clung to the pommel. With a toss of his magnificent head, Buccaneer downshifted into an energetic trot. His rider barely managed to hang on.

"You'd think she never rode before," Holly said.

"She hasn't," Kate said. "Not like this."

Angela hauled on the reins again. Buccaneer responded with a vigorous buck that catapulted Angela onto his neck. He got the bit between his teeth and thundered toward the brush jump.

"No!" Holly yelled.

At the last minute, Buccaneer swerved, and Angela flew off. She landed, sitting bolt upright, amid twigs and leaves.

Kate sprinted toward her. "Are you okay?"

"No." Angela spat out a dead leaf.

Jennifer ran up, pulling off her hoodie. She wrapped it around Angela's shoulders. Blood oozed from scratches on her bare midriff. One of her sandals had fallen off. Kate picked it up.

Sandals? What *was* Angela thinking?

At the far end of the arena, Buccaneer jammed on the brakes. He whirled around. Ears pinned, he trotted back toward them, head snaking along the ground.

"Watch out," Jennifer cried. "He's going to attack us."

Twigs snapped as Angela struggled to free herself from the brush jump. "Help me out."

"Don't move," Kate said. "I'll catch him."

"You can't," Jennifer said. "He's gone crazy."

"He's not crazy," Holly yelled. "He's angry." She tried again to reach them, but her wheels spun helplessly in the soft tanbark. "Kate, I already told you. Get the Life Savers."

Had she eaten the last one? Kate worried. *Had Buccaneer?* She couldn't remember. She pulled the pack from her pocket.

Yes! Three left.

Hand trembling, Kate held out the mints and walked toward Buccaneer, not feeling nearly as calm as she pretended to be. Suppose he barreled right past her and savaged Angela? She was his target. He didn't care about the others. They hadn't scared him and yanked on his sensitive mouth.

"Come here, boy," Kate said.

In three strides, Buccaneer shuddered to a stop, sides heaving with exertion. Thanks to Angela, he was in a complete lather. It would take at least an hour to cool him off.

"It's okay," Kate said. "Take it easy."

Through a tangle of forelock, Buccaneer eyed her cautiously. She opened her palm a little more, and one of the mints tumbled out. He swooped down and snarfed it up, then looked for more.

"Good boy," Kate said. "Good boy."

The words didn't matter. It was all in the voice. She'd learned that from watching countless videos about training horses. The barn fell silent. No sound from the others. Even Angela had stopped complaining. Another maxim shot through Kate's head.

Pretend you don't care.

She broke eye contact and looked the other way, as if it didn't matter whether she caught Buccaneer or not. He whickered, then pricked his ears and stepped toward her.

In one fluid movement, Kate reached for his reins.

6

STEAM ROSE FROM BUCCANEER'S sweat-covered rump and shoulders. Without being asked, Jennifer pulled his cooler off the side wing. "Want me to put it on?"

Kate nodded. "Thanks."

Smoothly, Jennifer unfurled it across Buccaneer's back. He fidgeted and flinched but didn't try to bolt. Kate fastened the front buckles, then checked his legs for injury. No heat or swelling, thank goodness. No sign of Liz, either. If everyone agreed to keep quiet, they could bury this mini-disaster without her ever finding out.

Kate looked at them. "Let's not tell Liz about this, okay?"

"My lips are sealed." Holly zipped a hand across her mouth.

"No problem," Jennifer said. "I'm cool with that."

Angela scowled. Her cuts and bruises appeared to be minor—nothing a few Band-Aids couldn't fix—but her pride had obviously taken a severe beating.

For a moment, Kate felt desperately sorry for her. This was Mrs. Dean's fault. She pushed Angela to win, no matter the cost. If it wasn't a horse show or a tennis tournament, it was ski racing. Last winter, in the junior slalom, Angela missed the gold medal by half a second and got yelled at for not trying harder.

"What do you say, Angela?" Kate said.

It was in their best interests to keep a mutual silence over this. She didn't want Liz to know about the jump, and Angela certainly wouldn't want to broadcast her massive flub-up.

"It's all *your* fault, Kate McGregor," Angela said.

Kate stepped back. "Mine? What did I do?"

"You got him riled up. If you'd ridden Buccaneer properly, he wouldn't have freaked out with me."

Holly gave a short bark of laughter. "You're delusional."

"You can't be serious," Kate said.

"No, I'm laughing my head off," Angela said. "Come on, Jen. Let's get out of here. I need a hot bath."

"Don't worry," Holly said, once they were out of earshot. "Angela won't say a word about this."

But Kate wasn't so sure.

* * *

Another storm woke Kate early the next morning. She burrowed into her pillow and tried to sleep, but the rain was too loud. Yawning, she got up and dressed quietly so as not to disturb Holly. They'd stayed up way too late, going over her exercises on the living room floor. Later, if it stopped raining, they'd try them out in the pool where, Holly insisted, they'd work much better.

After feeding the horses, Kate checked the whiteboard in Liz's office. It was divided into columns with riders' names, dates, and the horses they'd be riding written in red marker. Some were crossed out because Liz had postponed lessons for a week, but the beginner kids were still up there.

Kate counted three for this morning's group. *Good,* she thought, because that's all she could handle. Marmalade had pulled up lame, which left Snowball, Plug, and Daisy, an affable pinto mare who was slow enough for the younger children to ride. Kate took a closer look at the schedule, just to make sure.

Was that another name? If so, it had been reduced to a pinkish blur. So had the one beneath it. She'd written them in herself a couple of days ago, but obviously they'd cancelled and Liz had rubbed them out. Kate breathed a sigh of relief. Finding two more suitable horses, especially clean ones that didn't require hours of mud removal, would push her to the limit.

The phone rang and startled her.

Okay, so where was it?

Kate plunged into the chaos on Liz's desk. Feed catalogues, horse magazines, and invoices went flying. Some of Mrs. Dean's photos spilled from their box. Kate gathered them up.

The largest picture was tucked inside a clear sheet protector and showed a woman in a top hat and shadbelly coat standing beside a glossy chestnut. He had an arched neck and more braids than Kate had ever seen on one horse before. Behind them hung the British flag. Kate turned the picture over. On the back was written:

Caroline West & Rebel, Mexico City, 1968.

This had to be Jennifer's Olympic grandmother.

The phone stopped ringing, then started up again.

Kate finally found it on the floor jammed between Liz's spare riding boots and a box of worming medicine.

She snatched it up. "Hello."

"Timber Ridge?" said a man's voice.

"Yes."

"I'm looking for Liz Chapman," he said. "But she's not answering her cell phone."

With luck, Liz was still in bed. She'd stayed up even later than Kate and Holly, patching a pair of worn-out breeches and trying to balance the barn's checkbook.

Kate fumbled for a pencil. "I'll take a message."

"I'm from Meadow Park," he said. "Tell her there's been a delay. We won't be delivering Jennifer West's horse this weekend."

"So when's it coming?"

"Don't know," he said. "Our barn manager will call later with details."

Scribbling furiously, Kate hung up. She stuck her note to the wall above Liz's desk with a red pushpin, then scooted into the tack room to sort nosebands and locate missing girths.

Liz arrived moments before the kids.

Kate counted heads. *One, two, three . . . four?*

Whoops. Where did that last one come from? Kate

shot back into Liz's office and found her with yet another child, a little boy wearing a riding helmet several sizes too large. Now there were five, and she only had three horses ready.

Panic-stricken, she checked the whiteboard. So did Liz.

"This isn't right," Liz said, frowning. "Didn't you write down all the names, like I told you?"

"Yes, but—"

A shadow fell across the doorway, and Mrs. Dean loomed into view wielding a black umbrella. She shook it vigorously and sent a shower of raindrops all over Kate. "Liz, I hope you haven't forgotten that Marcia's having another lesson today."

Kate groaned. That made six.

Liz solved the problem by splitting the kids. She took three into the arena on their horses and left the others with Kate, learning how to take a bridle apart and put it back together again. After an hour, they switched groups, but this meant Liz had to teach for two hours rather than one. Her face looked grimmer than ever at the end of it.

She limped out of the indoor arena.

"I'm sorry for the muddle," Kate said. "I can't explain it."

"No harm done, this time," Liz said. "But don't let it happen again. I hate getting phone calls from irate parents."

* * *

When Kate got home, Holly was already in the pool. She'd put on a neoprene top to help her keep warm. While Kate studied the list of exercises, Holly swam laps, impatient to begin.

"It says here that you've got to re-educate your legs," Kate told Holly.

"Send them back to school?"

Kate grinned. "Art class," she said. "You're supposed to draw a mental picture of yourself walking."

"Du-uhh," Holly said. "I do that all the time. It's all I ever think about." She swam to the edge and hooked both elbows over the rim. "Well, that and riding my horse."

She also thought about Adam Randolph, a lot, but she wouldn't admit that to Kate because Kate liked him, too—even if she pretended not to.

Was it okay to mix boys and best friends?

Holly had no idea. Life in a wheelchair changed all the rules. One minute you're a seventh-grade track star;

the next you're stuck in the bleachers with a blanket over your lap, surrounded by kids and parents who try very hard not to stare at your legs.

"Pay attention," Kate said. "Exercise number one. Imagine your left foot is moving in a small circle, like this." She held up her leg and demonstrated.

Holly pursed her lips. "Okay. I'm imagining."

"Good," Kate said. "Now think about it really, really hard. Forget about the rest of you, and just focus on that foot. Try to remember what it used to feel like."

But no matter how hard Holly tried, she couldn't remember. Her stupid foot just hung there like a limp flounder dangling on a fishing line. She tried with her right foot, but nothing moved. The connection between her brain and her legs was broken.

"What's the next exercise?" she said.

"Knee bends," Kate said. "But maybe they'll work better if I move your legs first, to show them what to do." She pulled off her sweatshirt and slid into the pool.

With both hands, Kate grasped Holly's knees and moved them up and down, one at a time, the way they'd practiced the night before. Being in the water was supposed to help, but Holly knew it wasn't going to work, never mind what she'd said to Mom and Kate. But she had to do *something*. Sitting around in a wheelchair all day wasn't going to help her get better.

"Enough," she said, a few minutes later. "I can't feel a thing."

"You're giving up?" Kate said, shivering. Her lips were blue with cold. "We've only tried two exercises. There are tons more."

"It's not just two exercises," Holly said. "It's two *years*."

She pushed Kate away and swam to the deep end. Nobody, not even her best friend, could possibly understand how she felt, no matter how much they wanted to. Even the docs didn't understand why Holly couldn't walk. They said she had "hysterical paralysis."

Holly slapped the water with both hands. She hated that label. It made her sound like a helpless heroine in a Victorian novel, always fainting and being revived with smelling salts.

She dove underwater. At least down here, she wasn't such a freak. Her strong arms and shoulders made up for lack of leg power, and she swam two laps before resurfacing.

Kate crouched beside the ladder. "Ready to come out?"

This was another thing Holly hated. She couldn't even climb out of the pool by herself. It didn't have stairs—just an awkward metal ladder that worked for everyone else, but not her.

Sighing, she held up her arms. Kate hauled Holly from the pool, and she flopped onto the grass. "Thanks."

"Wanna talk about it?"

Holly tensed up. "What?"

"The accident," Kate said. She wrapped them both in a giant beach towel.

Tears sprang to Holly's eyes. She rubbed them furiously.

"You don't have to tell me if you don't want," Kate said.

"It's okay," Holly said. "I think I'm ready."

"Are you sure?"

It was now or never. She had to get this out there. She'd dodged around the issue with Mom, but Mom always cried and they never got around to talking about it . . . not properly, anyway. Maybe telling Kate would be easier.

"Dad and I were driving to the village, to get horse feed," Holly said, keeping her voice as steady as she could. "We stopped at a light. I was reading a book, on my new Kindle. I'd just gotten it for my birthday. There was a horrendous bang. It sounded like a monster was ripping the truck to bits. Then it rolled over and over—I don't know how many times—and I was thrown clear." She wiped away another tear. "I blacked out, just for a few seconds. When I opened my eyes, all I saw was a sheet of flame."

Kate gasped. "Oh, Holly."

She rushed on. "I tried to reach him, but I couldn't move. I could still see him, in the truck. The flames, it was—" She broke into a gut-wrenching sob. "I couldn't save him."

For what seemed like hours, they rocked back and forth. Kate held her so tight that Holly almost stopped breathing. Getting it all out was a huge relief, like letting go of a giant boulder she'd been lugging about for two years.

"It wasn't your fault," Kate whispered.

Holly sighed. "Keep telling me that."

AFTER HOLLY CRIED HERSELF OUT, Kate made them both hot chocolate. She carried two steaming mugs onto the back porch. Holly was sitting in the hammock, wrapped in a pink terrycloth robe. On her feet were matching bunny slippers, which made it quite clear they were through talking about the accident.

Kate handed one mug to Holly and sat down with the other.

"What happened this morning?" Holly said. "Mom told me you had too many kids and not enough ponies."

"I messed up the lesson schedule."

"C'mon, Kate," Holly said. "That sounds like something I'd do, not you. You're much too careful." She took a sip of cocoa. "Maybe Mom made a mistake. She's been forgetting stuff lately."

Kate had already thought of that and dismissed it. No, somebody—not she or Liz—had erased those names on purpose. But who? And why?

Unless . . .

Holly's eyes flashed. "I bet I know who it was."

The look on her face told Kate they were thinking exactly the same thing. The only person mean enough to pull a trick like this was Angela Dean.

"But Angela wasn't in the barn this morning," Kate said.

"So what? She could've done it yesterday. She was madder than a wet cat after getting dumped by Buccaneer."

Miserably, Kate agreed. "But why?"

"Revenge," Holly said. "And to make Mom mad at you."

"Well, she succeeded."

"Don't be silly," Holly said. "It takes a lot more than that to make my mother angry." She drained the last of her hot chocolate. "Are you going to tell her?"

"No."

"Why not?" Holly asked.

"Because I can't prove anything."

Holly set her empty mug on the table. "Just watch out, that's all. When Angela gets on the warpath, there's no stopping her."

* * *

Two hours later, Liz limped through the front door looking thunderous. She'd been at a committee meeting with Mrs. Dean, and that always put her in a bad mood.

Holly nudged Kate. "Uh, oh. Here comes trouble."

"You can say that again, young lady," Liz said.

She slammed her keys on the table and stumped toward them. Kate got off the couch to make room for her, but Liz parked herself in the wing chair.

"I want an explanation," she said, "so one of you had better start talking, and fast."

Kate looked at Liz, then at Holly. Had Angela blabbed to Mrs. Dean about getting tossed off Buccaneer? But that made no sense. The whole fiasco was her fault, and no matter how she spun it, she'd end up looking like an idiot.

"I'm waiting," Liz said.

"Mom," Holly said. "Kate told me about the lesson mix-up. You're not still mad over that, are you?"

Liz waved her off. "No, this one's far more serious." She leaned forward and pinned them both with her vivid blue eyes. "I've just been told by a very angry Mrs. Dean that you dared Angela to ride Buccaneer after getting him all steamed up just so that Angela would fall off and get hurt."

Kate opened her mouth, then closed it again. She sat down hard on the floor and slumped against the couch. Angela had surpassed herself this time. This story was so outrageous that it belonged in a comic book.

"That's insane," Holly said. "We'd never do that."

"But she did ride him, didn't she?" Liz's voice was dangerous.

The clock on Liz's mantel ticked off the seconds. A June bug crashed against the lampshade behind Kate and landed in her lap, upside down and waving its legs furiously. It looked as helpless as she felt.

"What did Mrs. Dean say?" Holly said.

"I want your version first," Liz replied.

They took turns and left nothing out, not even Kate's unplanned jump. "It wasn't Kate's fault, Mom. Buccaneer spooked and charged at the parallel bars. If she'd pulled him away, they'd have crashed into the wings." Holly took a deep breath. "You do believe me, don't you?"

Liz nodded slowly, still frowning.

"And then," Holly went on, "Angela showed up and said you'd given her permission to ride. Even Jennifer said so."

"And you let her?"

"No," Kate murmured. "I said to wait for you."

"But," Holly said, "Kate got off to help me, and Angela leaped into the saddle behind her back. She yanked at Buccaneer's mouth, and he galloped off like a wild thing."

"Then dumped her in the brush jump," Kate finished.

Surely Liz would believe them and not Mrs. Dean's ridiculous version, but her face was still angry. She struggled out of her chair, clamped on her crutches, and glared down at them like a vulture.

"Mom," Holly said. "Chill out. Angela got a few scratches, and the horse is okay. So what's the big deal?"

"The *big deal*, as you call it," Liz said, "isn't what happened. It's that you didn't tell me about it."

Miserably Kate said, "That's my fault. I told everyone not to."

"And I agreed," Holly said. "So did Jennifer."

Liz raised an eyebrow. "What about Angela?"

"I guess not," Holly said, looking mutinous. She stuck out her chin. "Look, Mom—"

"No, *you* look," Liz said. "Both of you. I'm not running a dude ranch here or pony rides at the beach. This is a working stable. We've got liability issues, and our insurance premiums will go through the roof if Mrs. Dean decides to sue."

Holly said, "She can't."

"Why not?"

"Because Angela's lying."

"I know she is," Liz said, "and I doubt Mrs. Dean would go through with it. But this doesn't alter the fact that you hid this from me. When Mrs. Dean blasted me tonight, I should've had an answer for her, right away, but I didn't."

"I'm sorry," Kate blurted. "I really am."

Liz looked at her. "And here's another thing I didn't know about. Jennifer West's horse. Seems you took a message and forgot to tell me."

"I left you a note," Kate said. "Honest."

"Where?"

"Above your desk. I stuck it up with a red pushpin."

"Not a good move," Holly said. "Mom's office is the pits. She wouldn't even find a tractor if you left one in there."

"That's enough, Holly," Liz said. "You should've told me, Kate. I felt like a complete idiot when Mrs. West called to follow up."

"*Lady* West," Holly muttered, but her mother didn't appear to have heard.

* * *

Robin and Sue were handling Saturday's barn chores, but Kate went over anyway. She wanted to find her note and show it to Liz. But all that remained on the red push-pin was a fragment of blue paper. The rest had been ripped off.

Had Angela struck again?

Kate aimed a vicious kick at Liz's rusty file cabinet. She wanted to scream with frustration, to bang her head against the wall. But what good would that do? The last thing Liz needed was Kate carrying on about pushpins and bits of missing paper.

All she could do was keep quiet and watch her back.

The way Holly said.

She heard a clatter of hooves. Robin led her dapple gray mare, Chantilly, down the aisle. Sue followed, leading Magician. The girls wore helmets and body protectors. Sue carried a crop, not that she'd need it with Holly's horse, but it was handy for opening gates and whacking at low branches.

"We're going trail riding," Robin said, pulling on her gloves.

Sue tightened Magician's girth. "Come with us."

"On what?"

"Buccaneer."

Fat chance of that, Kate thought, watching them mount and ride off. Liz had forbidden her to take Buccaneer on the trails. He was to be ridden only in the paddock or the indoor arena. And no more jumping either, Liz had warned, not until she'd had a chance to ride him again herself.

A voice behind her said, "What stall is Skywalker in?"

Kate turned to find herself staring at Jennifer West. The spiked hairdo was back, bright orange this time. Somehow, it suited her. No earrings, though—just a tiny gold stud in her left nostril. Kate blinked and looked again. She'd never been this close to a nose stud before.

"He's two stalls down from the feed room," she said, peering over Jennifer's shoulder. "Where's Angela?"

"At home," Jennifer said. "Nursing her cuts and bruises."

Kate winced. "I'm sorry she fell."

"So is she."

"Are you going to ride Skywalker?" Kate said.

Jennifer's green cargo pants ended at the knees. Not

exactly comfortable for riding. The stirrup leathers would cut right into her bare legs, and those striped socks wouldn't be much help, either.

"No, I'll just give him a brush-up," Jennifer said.

She whipped the purple bandana from her neck and knotted it around her forehead. It matched her sparkly nails—and her sparkly eye shadow. Kate made a mental note to share this with Holly—all the way from the rhinestones on Jennifer's purple tank top, right down to the purple laces that criss-crossed her black paddock boots.

Kate fetched Angela's grooming box from the tack room.

"Thanks," Jennifer said. "Wanna hang out while I brush?"

"Yeah, if that's okay."

"No worries," Jennifer said.

"You sound Australian," Kate said, puzzled. This girl changed accents faster than she changed her appearance.

Jennifer grinned. "I'm a Brit, but I've lived all over the world—Queensland, Paraguay, South Africa—you name it. My dad's a diplomat."

"I thought he trained dressage horses."

"He does that as well."

Head spinning with far-off places, Kate led the way to

Skywalker's stall. He greeted them with indifference. Bits of chewed wood clung to the whiskers on his lower lip. More were scattered across his rubber floor mat, and quite a few had made their way into a robin's nest that perched on the windowsill.

He'd been cribbing again.

"Poor thing," Jennifer said. "He's bored stiff."

Kate stood back to let her inside. Patches of dried mud dulled Skywalker's mahogany coat. His mane and tail bristled with burrs. Angela hadn't ridden him in almost a week, and who knew when she'd last groomed him.

"You take one side, and I'll take the other," Jennifer said, grabbing a curry comb. She tossed a dandy brush to Kate. "We'll have him fixed up in no time."

* * *

They took a break, and Kate asked Jennifer about her horse. He wasn't due to arrive for another week, and she had to be missing him like mad.

"He's part Trakehner and part Morgan," Jennifer said. "Dark chestnut with two white socks, and he loves vanilla pudding." She pulled a well-worn photo from one of her voluminous pockets. "Here he is. In my mum's kitchen."

"Kitchen?" Kate said. "With stoves and things?"

"Yup," Jennifer said, grinning. "It's even got a sink."

Kate stared at the photo. The horse had his nose in a blue-and-white striped mixing bowl held by a woman who looked like an older version of Jennifer. Her head was thrown back, and she was laughing at the camera.

"What's his name?" Kate said.

"Rebel."

It rang a bell. "Wasn't that your grandmother's horse?"

"My Rebel's a direct descendent," Jennifer said, counting on her fingers. "He's a great, great, yumpty-yump-great grandson. Dad gave him to me for my tenth birthday."

Kate felt a pang of envy. Her own father would be more likely to give her a box of butterflies. He'd just gotten an e-mail account and had sent her a detailed description of *heliconius melpomene*—a poisonous butterfly—and the phone number of his latest hotel in Brazil where she could reach him if necessary.

"Your father," Kate said. "Is he a—?" She stumbled over the words. "Angela said he was a *lord*."

"That's his first name," Jennifer said, laughing. "Short for Gaylord, but everyone calls him Lord."

8

HOLLY YELPED WITH GLEE over Kate's description of Jennifer. She demanded every detail, right down to the exact shade of Jennifer's nail polish.

"It was purple," Kate said. "And it sparkled."

"Grape or lavender?" Holly said.

"There's a difference?"

Holly gave a dramatic sigh. "You're worse than Mom."

"Where is she?" Kate hadn't seen Liz all day and wanted to give her an update. One of Skywalker's shoes was loose, and they were running low on sweet feed.

"She's at another meeting," Holly said. "Mrs. Dean's organizing a welcome party for Lord and Lady West, and—"

"Except he's not a lord," Kate said. "He's a—"

"Don't tell me," Holly said, holding up her hand. "He's a duke."

"Try again."

"A prince?"

Laughing, Kate shook her head and explained, then told Holly about Rebel and how he ate pudding from a bowl in Mrs. West's kitchen.

"Do you like her?" Holly said.

"Who? Mrs. West?"

"No, silly. Jennifer."

"Yeah. She's kinda cool."

"Well, I think she's weird, and her horse is, too." Holly spun away and headed for the kitchen. "I'm starving. Let's make some mac 'n' cheese."

Kate opened her mouth to argue, then changed her mind. Holly was right. Jennifer West *was* weird, but she was a good kind of weird, even if she did wear a nose stud.

* * *

On Monday morning, Liz announced the next riding team event, and, to Kate's relief, it included her and Buccaneer. They'd be performing a musical ride at the welcome party for Jennifer's parents. Rebel would arrive a few days earlier. In the meantime, Jennifer was to practice on Daisy.

"This'll be fun," Holly muttered. "Daisy won't even canter."

But Jennifer proved her wrong.

The pinto mare broke into a smooth canter, picking up the correct lead right away. Her ears flicked back and forth. Even her neck was arched, and, from what Kate could see, it looked as if Daisy was actually accepting the bit. If Jennifer could persuade lazy old Daisy to behave like this, she must be absolutely brilliant with her own horse. Liz would definitely put her on the team.

"I *told* you she could ride," Angela said, trotting beside her.

"She's good," Kate said, reluctantly. "*Very* good."

They'd been working in pairs for thirty minutes—Kate and Angela, Sue and Robin, and a self-confident Jennifer on her own, leading the group like a spearhead. She'd done musical rides before, and the others were supposed to be copying her moves.

It was like, all of a sudden, she'd become the star turn.

A week ago, nobody knew Jennifer existed—well, except for Angela—and now, here she was, showing them all how to ride serpentines, cross-overs, and a tricky wheel maneuver with her at its center. She even got Daisy to perform a turn on the forehand.

Kate's heart sank.

Her days on the team were over, no matter what Holly said about Liz not dumping her. The Timber Ridge riding team was for residents only, and Kate hardly qualified. As Angela so often pointed out, Kate was just an employee. Her moment of glory two weeks ago had been a one-shot affair that happened because Liz was in a jam and needed her. But with Sue riding Magician again and Jennifer West taking Denise's old place, the team wouldn't need Kate McGregor any more.

At least she had the musical ride.

Liz had put Holly in charge of the music. She was to call the maintenance department about upgrading the barn's loudspeaker system, then go through their own collection of CDs for something suitable.

"Tina Turner?" Holly said. "'Thriller'?"

"I was thinking Bach," Liz said. "Or the *1812 Overture*."

Holly groaned. "'Roll Over, Beethoven.'"

"What about 'William Tell'?" Robin said. "That's what the Mounties use. I've watched them on YouTube."

Sue fed Magician a carrot. "Isn't he some dude who shot an apple off his kid's head?"

"With a bow and arrow," Jennifer said, humming a few bars. She led Daisy into her stall and began rubbing her down.

For once, Kate noticed, the mare was actually sweaty.

*   *   *

Kate had just removed Buccaneer's saddle and bridle when Angela walked up with Liz's box of photos.

"Liz said you're to take this back to the house." She thrust it toward Kate.

Her arms were full and there was nowhere to put the box, except on the floor, and that wouldn't do. "Leave it in the tack room, okay? I'll pick it up it on my way out."

Angela shrugged. "Whatever."

"Be careful with it," Jennifer said, and popped her head over Daisy's door. "That picture of Gran is my dad's favorite, and it's the only copy we've got." She grinned at Kate. "That's why I chose it. Mum and Dad don't know about the party or the photo collage, and I bet they're going to be thrilled."

Today, Jennifer was back to normal. Well, more or less. Her hair had a faint orange glow, and there was a trace of purple glitter on one eyelid. Otherwise, she looked just like the rest of them—green t-shirts, buff breeches, and black boots. This would be their outfit for the musical ride, Liz said earlier, along with green helmet covers, green saddle pads, and green ribbons threaded into their horses' manes and tails.

"Like four-legged leprechauns," Holly had muttered.

With Robin's help, Kate finished up the barn chores and was halfway to the house when she remembered the photos. She ran back into the barn. Angela had left the box perched precariously on top of her saddle.

As Kate pulled the box down, it slipped from her grasp. Jennifer's grandmother fell out and landed behind Giles Ballantine's enormous tack trunk. With a mighty shove, Kate pushed it to one side, then stared with disbelief at the photo.

A big ugly crease ran right through Caroline West's head.

* * *

"I'm sorry, really sorry," Kate said over and over again. It felt like all she'd done for the past four days was apologize. First, there was her wild ride on Buccaneer, then the lesson mix-up and forgetting to tell Liz about Jennifer's horse, and now this.

Liz kept shaking her head.

"Mom, I can fix it," Holly said. "No problem."

"How?"

"With Photoshop. It'll look better than new."

"Wonderful," Liz said, with an edge of sarcasm. "But that's not the point." She glared at Kate. "You've wrecked an original photograph. How am I supposed to explain this to Mrs. Dean and Jennifer's mother?"

Kate sagged into a chair. She had no excuse, no explanation, other than that she'd been careless and in a rush.

"I'm sorry," she said again, feeling lame.

Liz lurched to her feet. She only needed one crutch now, but she looked mad enough to smash it over someone's head—Kate's, probably. "I'm going to the grocery store," she said. "And I'm thinking seriously of staying there."

The moment Liz left, Holly picked up the photograph, still in its clear plastic sleeve. She turned it over, then flipped it back and looked at it sideways.

"This wasn't your fault," she said.

Kate stared at her. "How'd you figure that?"

"Look at the cardboard backing," Holly said. "It's not creased."

"So?"

"Think about it," Holly said. "If this picture got damaged by falling behind that tack trunk, the cardboard would be creased, too." She paused. "But it's not, which means the picture was already messed up *before* it fell behind the trunk. Are you with me?"

Kate's head was spinning. "You mean—?"

"Yes," Holly said. "Somebody pulled that photo out of the plastic sleeve, creased it on purpose, then shoved it back inside."

"But who'd do that?"

Holly gave her a withering look. "Guess."

Suddenly, it all made sense—Angela with the box in her arms, then Jennifer saying the photo of her grandmother was the only one they had. Put that together with Angela's need for revenge, and . . . bingo!

"She got me again," Kate said. "Now what?"

"I fix the photo and make it look better than ever."

* * *

Holly scanned the battered photo into her laptop. Finally, here was something she could actually help with. All those solitary hours in front of a screen were about to pay off.

With Kate sitting beside her, Holly showed off her

91

skills. She manipulated healing brushes, filled the eye-dropper tool, and flourished Photoshop's magic wand. Pixel by pixel, the ugly crease disappeared.

"Amazing," Kate said. "You're a wizard."

Holy grinned. "Now, we'll brighten things up a bit."

After a few more mouse clicks, the faded colors burst into life. Rebel's coat gleamed, his rider's smile dazzled, and her yellow vest glowed like a buttercup.

"What do you think?" Holly said, feeling proud.

"Perfect."

Holly punched the print button, and out popped a sparkling new image. It really did look better than before. She also printed another with more muted colors that looked exactly like the original.

They'd beaten Angela at her own game.

"I could strangle her," Holly said.

"Me, too," said Kate. "But we can't say a word."

"Why not?"

"Because nobody would believe us," Kate said. "We have no proof, and Mrs. Dean will always take Angela's side, no matter what. She'd have to do something un-speakably awful to get in trouble with her mother."

"Like setting the barn on fire with her curling iron?"

"Don't even joke about it," Kate said.

* * *

While Kate helped Liz inside with the groceries, Holly waited for the right moment. Mom knew zilch about computers, and even less about Photoshop. She wouldn't have a clue about the magic Holly had just performed.

"I'm sorry for yelling at you," Liz said, when Kate handed her a glass of seltzer. "It was an unfortunate accident, but you've got to be more careful. We've had too many mishaps around here, lately."

"Shall I call Mrs. Dean to apologize?"

"I'll do it," Liz said. "We've got another meeting tomorrow."

Holly showed her the photos. "Here."

"Wow, you did a great job," Liz said. "These look way better than the old one."

"Told you," Holly said, feeling warm inside.

* * *

The riding team practiced every morning, accompanied by intermittent bursts of music from the loudspeakers and the banging of hammers on the barn roof. The repairs would be finished, Liz had been assured, in plenty of time for the big party.

It had morphed from a simple celebration into a full-blown pageant. There would be fireworks and dancing, old-fashioned games for the kids, such as hoops and hop-scotch, and a local pipe band for entertainment, to be fol-lowed later by a DJ disguised as Harry Potter. Mrs. Dean even wanted the riders to wear scarlet jackets and gold helmets with feathery plumes so they'd look like British Horse Guards.

But Liz vetoed it. "She'll have me dressed as Lady Godiva next," she grumbled.

"Or Boadicea," Kate said. "I bet we could whip up a chariot."

"And get Marmalade to pull it," added Jennifer.

Holly stiffened. All this fuss over Jennifer's parents! The stupid party had gotten out of control, and she'd lost interest in going. But Kate was totally caught up in it. When she wasn't schooling Buccaneer or mucking out stalls, she was working on new routines for the musical ride with Jennifer.

She'd even stopped ragging on Angela.

"We're part of the same team," Kate had said that morning, sounding faintly apologetic. "We've got to work together for your mom's sake."

Apart from the music, which took an hour, two at the most, Holly had nothing to do. Without Kate or Mom, she was trapped. She couldn't even swim, because getting out of the pool on her own was impossible.

Holly looked at her legs and hated them. She wanted to wear pretty shoes, to paint her toes ten different shades of pink and giggle when somebody tickled them. But most of all, she wanted to cram on her riding boots and ride Magician again.

Her cell phone buzzed.

It was probably Mom telling her to get something out of the freezer for dinner or maybe Kate with yet another bizarre description of Mrs. Dean's latest demands.

Holly flipped the lid and almost flipped out.

I'M GOING 2 THE PARTY. R U?

Grinning, she tapped a reply and began to plan her outfit.

9

KATE RAN ALL THE WAY home from the barn. She burst through the kitchen door and found Holly at the table, slathering two slices of bread with peanut butter and honey.

"I've got great news," Kate said, breathing hard.

Holly licked her fingers. "Me, too."

Kate threw herself into a chair and pulled off her boots. They were fine for riding, but not for running. She peeled off both socks as well. The beginnings of a blister bubbled on her left heel. "Okay, you first."

"Adam's coming to the party."

"Awesome," Kate said. That blister was going to cause trouble. She got up to rummage in the cupboard for a box of Band-Aids. There had to be one in here, somewhere.

"Really?" Holly said. "You're not just saying that?"

"No, really," Kate said, still rummaging.

"So, what's your news, then?" Holly said.

Kate found a roll of plaster, ripped off a strip, and stuck it over her heel. That would have to do. "Liz said I could take Buccaneer on the trails." She put her socks back on. "I can jump the hunt course, as well."

"Cool," Holly said. "What'll you wear for the party?"

"I dunno." Kate hadn't even thought that far ahead. "Shorts and a t-shirt, I guess."

"Bo-o-oring," Holly said. "I'm going to wear a long skirt and a camisole with skinny straps, and Mom's turquoise earrings, and a shawl I found in her closet. It's from Spain, I think, and it's got this superfantastic fringe, and"—she sucked in her breath—"I'm gonna shave my legs."

"Why bother?" Kate said. "Nobody will see them."

The light left Holly's eyes. "Never mind," she said and jerked her wheels so hard that they made skid marks on the vinyl floor.

Kate put a hand to her mouth. "Oh, I'm so—"

"Forget it." Holly zoomed out of the kitchen.

In a flash, she was gone.

"I'm sorry," Kate yelled after her, but it was too late. In the distance, their bedroom door slammed shut.

* * *

Kate stared at the bread and the smears of peanut butter and made herself a sandwich. It tasted like sawdust.

She was Holly's best friend, and she'd just made fun of her legs. She hadn't meant to, but that's the way it came out. She'd been thoughtless and stupid, and, oh, how she wanted to take those horrible words back and pretend she'd never said them.

Sweat trickled down Kate's forehead. She wiped it off with the back of her hand. Through the screen door, she could see the pool—blue and cool and inviting—and realized she'd not been in it for days. Neither had Holly. She couldn't swim without help.

Kate washed down her last bite with a slug of milk, then dashed along the hall. She banged on the bedroom door.

"Holly, open up. Let's go for a swim."

Nothing. Not even breathing.

She banged again. "Look, I'm sorry. I can't believe I said that."

"Go away."

Grabbing the door knob, Kate twisted it hard.

"Don't bother," said Holly's voice. "It's locked."

Kate yanked away her hand as if scalded. Locking doors was an absolute no-no. If something awful happened, like a fire, and Holly was locked in a room by herself, they'd have to break the door down, and by then it might be too late.

Kate gulped. "But you're not allowed to—"

"I don't care. Just leave me alone."

The house phone rang. Kate waited for Holly to answer. But the line kept on ringing, so Kate raced back to the kitchen and snatched up the receiver.

"Hello?"

Robin's voice said, "Liz has given us the afternoon off, so I'm going trail riding with Sue, up to the lake. We'll take the horses swimming. Wanna come with us?"

"Yeah," said Kate, feeling a twinge of guilt over Holly.

"Bring a bathing suit," Robin said, and hung up.

The only suit Kate had was in the bedroom she shared with Holly, and no way would she knock on the door and ask for it. She'd just have to watch the others swim, that's all.

Magician adored the water. He'd probably lie down

and roll in it, and Chantilly would paw and splash, but Kate had no idea how Buccaneer felt about getting wet. Some horses hated it.

Kate climbed back into her boots and grabbed a pack of Life Savers, then took off for the stables. On the roof, two workmen swung hammers; another carried shingles up a ladder. He tossed a cigarette butt onto the ground. Kate stomped on it. Smoking at the barn was absolutely forbidden.

Buccaneer, along with Marmalade and Plug, was cropping grass in the paddock. He saw Kate coming and trotted to the gate. She fed him a mint, clipped a lead to his halter, and led him into the run-in shed. It was just a row of four stalls with outside doors beneath an over-hang, but Buccaneer seemed more settled here, away from all the noise.

Kate fetched a body brush and curry comb from the biggest stall, which was used as a tack and feed room. Sometimes, when the main barn got overwhelmed with little kids, the older girls would sneak up here and hang out. They'd sprawl on the tattered old couch and read dusty copies of *Seventeen* and *Young Rider* or gossip about whoever wasn't there.

Mrs. Dean wanted to spruce the whole place up and

turn it into a proper teen clubhouse, but, so far, the girls had overruled her. Even Angela, for some odd reason, liked it up here. Her lime green iPod dangled from a loose socket on the wall. Kate unplugged it, then got busy grooming Buccaneer.

But no matter how hard she brushed, Kate couldn't shake off the awful way she'd treated Holly. Should she call and apologize again? She'd forgotten to bring her cell phone, so that would mean calling from Liz's office, with Sue and Robin hanging about and maybe others as well. Better not.

She saddled Buccaneer and rode down to the barn.

Daisy was tied to a hitching post outside. The mare had serious grass stains on her belly, and Jennifer was rinsing her off with a garden hose. Kate kept her distance. Buccaneer didn't seem too keen on the hose. He tossed his head and eyed it warily like it was a snake.

"Hi, Jen," Kate said.

No reaction. Jennifer dipped her brush into a bucket of soapy water and began to scrub Daisy's foreleg.

Maybe she hadn't heard.

"Hi," Kate said, a little louder. "I'm going on the trails with Sue and Robin. Would you like to come with us?"

"No," Jennifer said, and went on scrubbing.

That was it. Nothing more, not even a smile.

For a moment, Kate just sat there. This wasn't like Jennifer at all. She was always full of chitchat. Sometimes, you couldn't get her to shut up—like this morning, when she talked about Rebel non-stop during team practice. He was due to arrive at any time, and Jen had been bubbling with excitement.

"Hurry up," Sue yelled. "We're waiting."

* * *

They rode the narrow trails in single file, ducking low branches and avoiding rocks. Buccaneer snorted and shied at a boulder, then almost jumped out of his skin when a squirrel darted across the path.

Behind her, Robin laughed. "Horses are only afraid of two things," she said, "things that move and things that don't."

"Good one," Sue called out.

Kate forced herself to relax. The more she tensed up, the worse Buccaneer behaved. He was jiggling about like a jack-in-the-box by the time they reached the hunt course—a line of rustic fences low enough for Plug and Snowball to scramble over.

She'd jumped it many times with Magician. They'd

also jumped the more challenging cross-country course, and she longed to try it with Buccaneer. He was ready— she knew it—but Liz disagreed.

"Just the hunt course," she'd insisted.

Sue and Magician went first. They blasted over the jumps as if they were no bigger than shoe boxes. Robin followed, a little more sedately, on Chantilly.

"Your turn," Sue yelled. "Let him go."

Buccaneer needed no urging. He raced at the first fence—a simple cross-rail between two pine trees—and jumped so high, Kate thought they'd crash into the branches overhead. Then came the brush jump, and he leaped over that like a kangaroo. One by one, the jumps flew by—logs, a double oxer, and another brush. He cleared them all with ease.

"That was fantabulous," Sue said. "How about the cross-country course? I bet he'd be amazing."

Kate shook her head. "Not allowed."

"Then let's go for a swim," Robin said.

They trotted toward the lake, little more than a large pond with a tiny beach and willow trees that dipped their long graceful boughs into the water. Buccaneer wouldn't go anywhere near it. He snorted and fussed and dug his toes in the sand.

Sue stripped down to her bathing suit and then removed Magician's saddle and bridle, leaving just his halter on. She vaulted on his back and rode him into the pond. Within minutes, his legs buckled and he collapsed with an enormous sigh. Laughing, Sue threw herself clear just in time. Robin and Chantilly paddled happily at the water's edge.

Watching them splash about, Kate felt a surge of envy. It would've been nice to wear a bathing suit, or at least a pair of shorts, instead of her breeches and sweaty riding boots.

Immediately, she felt guilty.

At least she was out here and not trapped in a wheelchair, unable to go much of anywhere unless someone took you. Tomorrow, after team practice, she'd spend the rest of the day with Holly. They'd do whatever she wanted. They could try on outfits for the party—it was only three days away—and experiment with makeup, then laugh at themselves posing in front of the mirror. Holly loved all this girly-girl stuff. Kate didn't know one end of a mascara brush from the other.

Maybe now was the time to find out.

She was still deep in thought when Sue and Robin came back. Magician shook himself vigorously and sprayed Kate with water. It felt good to cool off.

"Is anything wrong?" Sue pulled a towel from her knapsack and wrapped it around her shoulders. "You look kinda, I dunno, bummed out."

Kate shrugged. "I've been a jerk, and Holly's mad at me."

"She's not the only one," Robin said quietly.

"What do you mean?"

Robin and Sue exchanged a quick glance. "We weren't going to say anything," Sue said, "but—"

All Kate's alarm bells went off at once.

"It's Angela," Robin said.

Kate braced herself. "Okay, tell me."

"This morning, after you went home for lunch," Sue said, rubbing her wet hair, "Angela started showing off to Jennifer about the Hampshire Classic. They were hanging out in the tack room. I guess they didn't realize that Robin and me were in Tilly's stall and could hear them."

"What did she say?"

"She told Jen you cheated," Sue said, "that you double-crossed the team, and if it hadn't been for her brilliant riding, we'd have lost the challenge cup."

Kate's mouth fell open in astonishment.

Was there no end to Angela's lies? It was *Angela* who'd cheated. She messed up Magician's stall moments before the judges came by, then moved the course markers so Kate would get lost in the woods. And right before the show jumping, she fiddled with Kate's stirrup. It flew off as she was going over the parallel bars. The only competition Angela didn't interfere with was dressage, probably because she couldn't figure out a way to do it without being caught.

Despite the heat, Kate shivered. "What else did she say?"

"She said Liz would be dumping you from the team once the party was over." Robin sat down beside Kate. "She also told Jennifer that you didn't belong at Timber Ridge and that nobody liked you."

No wonder Jennifer had snubbed her.

"It wasn't me who cheated," Kate said. "It was Angela."

But she couldn't prove it. She'd kept quiet and not told anyone about her suspicions. Only Holly knew what dirty tricks Angela had pulled at the three-day event. The team won, anyway, but Kate lost the individual gold medal, thanks to Angela Dean.

10

KATE RODE OFF BY HERSELF. Robin and Sue wanted to go with her, but she needed time alone to calm down. She'd never been this angry before. All she could think about was getting her own back, but how? She thought long and hard and came up with nothing.

Why did Angela do this?

What had Kate ever done to her?

Nothing, Holly had said. Angela always went ballistic when someone else stole the limelight. She had to be the star, all the time. Her mother insisted on it.

So where did that leave Jennifer, Kate wondered, as she trotted Buccaneer through the woods. Riding Daisy the way she did, Jennifer had already proved she was a better rider than Angela. Maybe, once the honeymoon was over, Jennifer West would become Angela's next victim.

The trail narrowed and Kate saw two riders coming toward her. Robin and Sue? But that was impossible. She'd left them at the lake ten minutes ago, still in their bathing suits and planning another swim.

Kate slowed to a walk and looked again. No, it was Angela in a bright yellow t-shirt. But who was she with? It couldn't be Jennifer because that wasn't Daisy or any other horse in the barn.

They rode closer.

Oh, wow. It could only be Rebel, and he was stunningly gorgeous—bright chestnut, two white socks, and a mane that went on forever. Just like Buccaneer's.

A few yards away, Angela halted. "Well, look who's here."

"Yeah." Jennifer gave Kate a cold stare.

"She's all alone," Angela said, with a smirk. "I guess nobody wants to ride with her any more. Isn't that a pity."

It took all Kate's willpower not to smack Angela's silly face with her riding crop. She gripped Buccaneer's reins even tighter, which made him more fidgety than ever. He pinned his ears and grunted.

"That horse is dangerous," Angela said. "He's a menace."

"So are you," Kate shot back. "Now get out of my way." If she stuck around for one more second, she'd be tempted to do something really dumb.

But Angela blocked the path. "Make me."

Kate looked around wildly. To her left was that wretched boulder Buccaneer had shied at. There was no way he'd go past it without crowding Skywalker or kicking out at him. He didn't like Angela's horse any more than he liked her. On the right, a winding path led deeper into the woods.

It was her only way out.

Without thinking, she took it. But after only a few moments, Kate realized her mistake. This trail was part of the cross-country course, and around the next corner lay a nasty ditch that was always full of stagnant water.

She'd be lucky to get Buccaneer within ten feet of it.

Sure enough, he slid to a stop, then skittered sideways into the undergrowth and narrowly missed a tree stump. Brambles tore at Kate's arms. Low-hanging branches almost knocked her helmet off. Heart thumping, she steered Buccaneer back onto the trail. Luckily, they wound up on the other side of the ditch.

Angela splashed through it, then jerked Skywalker to

a halt inches away from Buccaneer's nose. "You're a coward, Kate McGregor, and so is your vicious horse."

"I'll match him against yours any day." The words were out before she could stop them.

Jennifer rode up. "Why don't you race?" she drawled.

"That's a great idea," Angela said. Her eyes glittered. "We could use the cross-country course, except Kate's too chicken to ride it."

All Kate's good intentions vanished. She had blood streaming down one arm, and that heel blister was killing her. Plus she'd had more than enough of Angela's venom. It was time to get even, and she'd break all the rules to do it.

"You're on," she said.

A triumphant look flashed across Angela's face. "Now we'll see who's the best rider."

* * *

They lined up, side-by-side, in front of the first jump. This was wrong—unbelievably wrong—but Kate didn't care. She wanted to race Angela, and she wanted to beat her.

"Go!" Jennifer yelled.

Angela plunged ahead first, so close to Kate that Skywalker's hindquarters bumped Buccaneer's left shoulder. But Kate had anticipated this and checked her horse before he stumbled. Three strides in front, Angela zoomed over the post-and-rail fence. Buccaneer followed, straining to take the lead, but Kate held him back. He needed to conserve energy. They had nine more jumps and a mile of challenging terrain to cover.

"Easy, boy," she said, as they cleared the next fence— parallel bars with a steep bank on the other side. In front, she could see Angela, hunched over Skywalker's neck, whipping him forward with a reckless regard for the rough footing. Kate began to question her impulsive decision.

What if Buccaneer fell and hurt himself?

Angela disappeared around a bend, and Kate's heart sank. Next up was the ladder—an easy jump with three horizontal poles—but beyond it lay the water hazard.

Was there a way around it? Kate couldn't remember.

"One, two, three, . . . and up," she counted.

They flew over the ladder, and Buccaneer jerked to a bone-crunching halt. Somehow, Kate managed to stay in the saddle, but only just. She was still pulling her wits together when Angela's voice pierced the silence.

"You'll never catch me now."

She had two options: Admit defeat, or figure out a way to get Buccaneer over the stream. It wasn't wide. He didn't even have to wade through it. A short leap would do the job.

Beads of fresh blood welled on her arm. Kate fumbled in her pocket for a tissue, but her fingers found Life Savers instead.

Of course.

She slid to the ground and fed Buccaneer a mint.

He crunched it down and looked for more. Good, at least he wasn't freaking out over the water. Slowly, Kate bribed him closer with mint after mint until they reached the edge.

So far, so good.

Kate released one of the clips that secured Buccaneer's reins to his snaffle and carefully slid the single rein over his neck and into her hand. Gripping it firmly, Kate jumped across the stream. The rein reached, but only just. She turned and leaned toward Buccaneer, coaxing him with the remaining mints.

"Come on, boy, you can do it."

Buccaneer trembled. He eyed her warily from beneath his forelock. He jigged from side to side, then airlifted off the ground like a startled stag—all four feet at once—and landed beside her with a mighty *whump.*

"Way to go," Kate said, patting his sweaty neck.

Greedily, he vacuumed up his reward.

Kate reattached his reins and swung herself into the saddle. How much time had they lost? Angela would be far ahead by now, and there was little hope of catching her.

* * *

The woods spilled into a large, sloping meadow. Overhead, cables creaked and metal seats swung in the breeze. Lift towers marched up the middle in single file. This was the ski area's bunny hill.

Kate gave Buccaneer his head, and they galloped across the meadow. She leaned forward, into his flying mane, and wondered what had happened to Jennifer. If she had any sense, she'd be walking Rebel slowly back to the barn. He'd just endured two hundred miles in a horse trailer, and he'd be stiff and sore.

A flash of color caught her eye. Angela's shirt?

No, it was a yellow sign with black letters, warning skiers about rocks and unmarked obstacles. Buccaneer snorted and danced sideways. Kate guided him to the right, back into the woods, and followed the small red triangles that marked the cross-country course. A line of fresh hoof prints scarred the soft ground.

How far ahead was Angela?

Picking up speed, Kate jumped a rustic gate, then flew over the railroad ties and veered left toward the palisade—a solid board fence that spanned the width of the trail. On both sides, thorn bushes formed a dense barricade.

And there was her rival, stuck in front of it.

Skywalker was dodging from left to right like a quarterback. Skidding and sliding, he whipped in circles. Stones flew from his hooves. Flecks of foam dotted his sweaty shoulders. Angela laid into him with her spurs and riding crop.

"Get on, you lazy horse," she screamed.

Kate winced. Poor Skywalker. His push-buttons had obviously failed. She gave him a wide berth and aimed Buccaneer at the fence, keeping as close as possible to the edge. There was plenty of room for two horses to jump at the same time, providing both riders paid attention.

"Heads up," she hollered. "Coming through."

Buccaneer didn't even hesitate. Ears pricked, he soared over the palisade like he'd just sprouted wings. Within moments, Kate heard hoof beats, thundering up behind her.

She took a quick glance backward.

Angela was gaining fast. Either she'd cheated and gone around the jump, or Skywalker had been shamed into jumping it by Buccaneer's brave performance. Kate didn't dare push any faster. The footing was too rough, littered with twigs and small stones. Angela drew level. For a split second, their eyes locked. Angela shot Kate a malevolent look, then surged ahead.

The trail forked.

To the left, lay the last three obstacles of the cross-country course. But Angela peeled off to the right, down a short hill, and into a large, open field. It had just been cut for hay, so the grass was short. Buccaneer wanted to run, and Kate let him. With a burst of energy, he lengthened his stride and galloped past Skywalker.

She was going to win.

She *had* to win, she realized with a shock. If Angela beat her, she'd tell everyone, including Liz, and Kate would be in even more hot water. The only way to keep Liz from finding out about the race was to win it.

Angela wouldn't say a word if she lost.

11

KATE AND BUCCANEER INCREASED their lead. One more obstacle lay between them and victory—a crumbling stone wall that meandered along the property line. Mrs. Dean said it was an eyesore and would be replaced with white board fencing, but right now Kate was glad it hadn't been.

She glanced behind her. Skywalker was tiring fast. Despite Angela's best efforts, they were a good ten lengths away. The wall drew closer. Kate lined herself up with the safest place to jump—a low section with no loose rocks on the ground to sabotage her takeoff.

"We can do it," she whispered into Buccaneer's flying mane.

They were riding west, into the late afternoon sun.

On top of the wall, something glinted. A shiny stone? Glass? Kate scrunched up her eyes. There it was again, and it was wire—*barbed* wire—coiled like a snake and ready to strike.

Panic stricken, Kate hauled on the reins. She threw everything she had to one side, and Buccaneer swerved away at the last minute like a cutting horse.

"Angela," she yelled. "Don't jump."

But her words were lost in the wind. Angela either didn't hear or chose not to. She whacked Skywalker with her crop and charged full-tilt at the wall.

No, she couldn't be this *stupid.*

All the breath left Kate's body. Her heart lodged itself somewhere between her neck and mouth as she watched Angela ride Skywalker over the deadly wire like a steeplechase jockey.

* * *

Miserably, Kate scanned the stone wall, looking for a break to scramble through. Guilt and shame engulfed her, not because she'd lost the race, but because she'd lost her temper and taken an unforgivable risk with a valuable horse.

Angela's scorn rang in her ears. "I beat you, Kate McGregor. You're too chicken to jump a *real* fence."

Skywalker's coat glistened with sweat. His sides heaved, his nostrils flared in and out like miniature bellows. It'd be a miracle if he didn't pull up lame after this. It'd be an even bigger miracle if Buccaneer didn't either. Kate slid off his back and ran her hands over his legs. No sign of heat, but she'd hose him down anyway—if he'd let her.

With a triumphant laugh, Angela galloped off and Kate trudged back to the barn. Her anxiety level rose with every step. Angela wouldn't waste a moment telling everyone, including Liz, she'd beaten Kate on the cross-country course.

* * *

News of Angela's victory spread through the barn like poison ivy. Even the little kids snickered and whispered behind their hands. By mid-afternoon the next day, Liz found out.

"Is this true?" she said, cornering Kate in the kitchen. "Or is Angela making it all up?"

"Mom, what are you talking about?" Holly said.

Kate gulped. She'd not shared her insane ride with Holly. They were still smarting over yesterday's hurtful words and being super-polite to one another.

"It seems Kate ignored my instructions," Liz said.

"She raced Angela on the cross-country course, flat out, all the way."

"Who won?" Holly said.

"That's hardly the point," Liz snapped. She turned on Kate. "Why did you race? On Buccaneer, of all horses?"

"I'm sorry," Kate blurted. "I didn't think."

She had no excuse, no ready explanation. If she told Liz the truth about Angela's dirty tricks, Liz would bawl her out for not speaking up sooner. Then she'd confront Mrs. Dean, who'd support her daughter to the hilt, and Liz would have to back down. If she didn't, her job might be in jeopardy. Mrs. Dean ruled Timber Ridge like a medieval queen. She made the decisions about who ran the ski area, the tennis club, and the stables.

"You're grounded," Liz said. "Keep away from the barn."

"But, Mom," Holly protested. "What about your foot?"

"I can manage without Kate's help."

Liz's words cut like a knife. Kate felt tears springing to her eyes. Angrily, she wiped them away. "I'd better move back to Aunt Marion's."

"You can't," Holly cried. "You'll miss the musical ride."

"She won't," Liz said. "I'm only grounding her for

two days." Her voice softened. "Look, Kate. I don't want to be mean or unfair, but you've let me down. I don't feel I can trust you any more. It's been one thing after another, and—"

"Mom, it's not her fault," Holly said. "It's Angela. She's a bratface, and I hate her."

"That's enough, Holly."

The phone rang. Liz answered it and frowned. "Yes, we're coming. We'll be there in ten minutes." She plucked her purse off the counter and grasped the handles of Holly's wheelchair.

"Where are we going?" Holly said.

Liz pushed her toward the door. "Your physical therapy appointment. I'd forgotten all about it."

"Can we go shopping after?"

Liz nodded, then turned and shot Kate a look that said, quite clearly, *See if you can stay out of trouble till we get back*.

* * *

For twenty minutes, Kate roamed the empty house in a turmoil of defiance and self-pity. She wanted to tell Liz exactly what Angela had been up to, but it was far too late. No matter what she said, it'd only look like a bunch of lame excuses.

At least Holly had stuck up for her. That meant she was ready to patch things up. Kate had tried the night before, but Holly was as prickly as her name. She'd spent the evening helping Liz with the photo collage while Kate wrote a dutiful e-mail to her father.

All of a sudden, she missed him fiercely.

She wanted to hear his voice, like right now. The time difference with Brazil was two hours. Perfect. She'd catch him at dinner. He wouldn't understand her woes, but he'd listen, even if it was with only half an ear.

Kate reached for her cell phone but her back pocket was empty. She tried the side ones. Not there, either. She tipped everything out of her knapsack, scoured Holly's bedroom, and peered beneath the couch. No luck.

Then she remembered.

Her phone was in the pocket of her blue windbreaker. She'd worn it to the barn that morning. Okay, so where was it? Kate raced back into the room she shared with Holly, but her jacket wasn't strewn across her bed or stuffed in the closet. It wasn't on the hook in the laundry room, either, or flung carelessly over the porch railing.

There was only one place it could be . . . the barn.

Kate glanced at the kitchen phone. Would Liz have a fit if she ran up long-distance charges to Brazil? Better not risk it. She was in enough trouble already.

It would take less than five minutes to fetch her jacket. She could run all the way there and back, and Liz would never know. And if someone saw her, so what? Nobody else knew she was grounded.

Holly's laptop was on the kitchen table. Kate fired it up, clicked her dad's e-mail, and wrote his number on a pink sticky. It had her name and a Thelwell pony cartoon at the top. Kate tucked the note in her t-shirt pocket, then grabbed a roll of Life Savers. Maybe she could sneak in a quick visit to Buccaneer as well.

The barn was quiet, except for Angela and Jennifer gushing over Rebel in his stall next to Daisy. The other horses had been turned out. Kate retrieved her windbreaker from Liz's office. Her phone, thank goodness, was still in the pocket. She'd call Dad on her way back to the house.

But first, she had a few peppermints to share.

Outside, the builders had left a mess. Rotting lumber, bent nails, and paper coffee cups lay beside a pile of musty hay. Cigarette butts were scattered about. Kate spotted a crumpled Marlboro pack. She stuffed it in her t-shirt pocket, then kicked at the butts to bury them in the dirt.

There was a red glow. Something flared and flickered,

and before Kate could react, tongues of flame licked upward and devoured the hay. It happened so fast that she was rooted to the spot. Then common sense overtook fear, and she raced for the hose.

Kate aimed the nozzle and let loose a jet of water.

"What are you doing?" Angela yelled.

"Fire!" Kate yelled back. "Get the other hose."

Jennifer moved faster. Amid clouds of billowing smoke, she helped Kate reduce the smoldering inferno to a pile of soggy embers. Breathing hard, Kate leaned forward and dropped the hose. The empty pack of Marlboros fell from her pocket.

Angela swooped to pick it up. "What's this?"

"Give me that," Kate said. "I'll throw it away."

"No, you won't," Angela said. "It's evidence."

* * *

It took another ten minutes before Kate was satisfied the fire was well and truly out. This left no time to visit Buccaneer. He'd have to wait until Sunday for his mints. She'd give him a double ration after they finished the musical ride.

Kate raced back to the house. Her father's e-mail was still open on Holly's laptop. Kate punched in his number and got a hotel clerk in Rio de Janeiro who didn't understand English very well. Speaking slowly, Kate asked him to ring her father's room, but there was no answer. She left a message with the clerk.

Dad call me. I miss you.

After washing her hands and face, Kate turned on the TV. Children in Haiti were starving, floods in Indonesia had left thousands homeless, and a volcano was spewing lava in Peru. Her own problems seemed petty and miniscule, but they were *her* problems and she had to deal with them.

At six-thirty, Liz and Holly rolled through the back door. Holly grinned at Kate and held up a shiny white bag with blue tissue paper poking out the top like bunny ears.

"Got some cool stuff," she said. "Wanna see it?"

"Sure."

Holly upended her bag. Lip gloss, eye shadow, and nail polish—all pink and sparkly—spilled across the kitchen table, followed by pink razors and a bottle of strawberry body lotion. Holly squirted a glob of pink gooey stuff on Kate's arm.

Rubbing it in, Kate ooh'd and aah'd. Sharing loot was Holly's way of saying things were going to be okay between them. But Kate's heart wasn't in it. She'd admire it all properly later. First, she had to tell Liz about the fire and was wondering how to begin when the phone rang.

Maybe it's Dad, Kate thought. She grabbed the phone, then slumped against the wall.

"Yes, she's here. Please hold on a minute." She put her hand over the receiver and turned to Liz. "It's Mrs. Dean."

"Thanks." Liz took the phone.

Keeping a wary eye on Liz, Kate pulled up a chair next to Holly. Her mother's mouth had hardened into a straight line, and frown lines creased her brow. Had Angela invented yet another wild story? Well, whatever it was, Kate didn't care. She wasn't going to hide stuff any more. As soon as Liz's phone call was over, she'd come clean about going to the barn.

She nudged Holly. "How did the therapy go?"

"No change," Holly said, holding up an eyelash curler. "I might walk again, I might not." She wrinkled her nose. "What's that disgusting stink?"

Kate sniffed. All she smelled was strawberry body lotion.

"Smoke," Holly said. "You smell like a—"

Liz's angry voice drowned Holly's words. "What did you say?"

"Uh, oh," Holly said. "I smell trouble."

Kate took a deep breath. This time, she would not back down. Yes, she'd disobeyed Liz and gone to the barn, but if she hadn't, that fire would've consumed it and the horses as well. There was no way Liz could slam her for this.

Still frowning, Liz drummed her fingers on the counter. Mrs. Dean's disembodied voice reverberated around the room, squawking like the unseen teacher in a Charlie Brown cartoon. Liz grimaced and held the phone away from her ear.

"Yes, thank you," she said. "I'll take care of it."

Slowly, she turned her thunderous face toward Kate.

12

HOLLY STRUGGLED FOR BREATH, like she'd somehow gotten trapped inside a wet sleeping bag. She looked from Mom to Kate and back again. Mom's face had turned pale the way it always did when she was unspeakably angry.

"What's wrong? Holly said.

Kate cut in. "Liz, I can explain."

"Not this time," Liz said. She lurched away from the counter and stood over Kate, shaking her head. "There's no explanation for what you've just done."

"Done what, Mom?"

"Kate went to the barn," Liz said. "Right, Kate?"

"Yes, but—"

"And there was a little fire, right?"

Holly gasped. Barn fires were the worst. All that wood and dry hay. Fires spread fast and killed animals within minutes.

"Are the horses okay?" she said.

Stupid question. If they weren't okay, Mom wouldn't be standing here right now. She'd be out the back door and racing for the barn. Holly shivered. Fire scared her witless. She even flinched whenever anyone lit a match.

"Yes," Liz said. "The horses are safe. Angela and Jennifer got there just in time to put the fire out." She bent closer to Kate. "Why don't you take it from here?"

"It was the builders," Kate said.

Holly tried to catch her eye, but Kate looked away.

"They left a mess," Kate said, stumbling over her words. "Coffee cups and cigarette butts all over the place. I was trying to make sure they were all out when a pile of hay went up in flames. So I grabbed the hose, and then Jennifer got the other one, and we—" She let out a huge sigh. "I'm sorry for going to the barn, but if I hadn't—"

"We wouldn't have had a fire in the first place," Liz finished.

"No." Kate shook her head violently. "I put it out."

"Wrong," Liz said. "You started it."

There was an awful silence.

Kate's eyes opened wide. "It was an accident. The builders—"

"Yes, I know about the builders," Liz said. "They smoked, and I told them not to. But you, Kate, of all people, ought to know better than to smoke around a horse barn."

"Me?"

"You were smoking, and you started a fire."

Holly could hardly believe what she was hearing. "Mom, I—"

"Stay out of this Holly."

"Liz, I wasn't smoking," Kate said. "I *hate* cigarettes."

"Marlboros, wasn't it?" Liz said, sounding dangerous. "Red-and-white pack, filter tips?"

"Yes," Kate said. "I found it on the ground by the rubbish and the hay. I was going to throw it out, but Angela took it." She looked up at Liz. "That pack wasn't mine."

"I'm afraid it was."

"How do you know?" Holly said, unable to stop herself.

Her mother's eyes narrowed. "It had Kate's name on it."

"What?" Holly clamped a hand to her mouth. If

she'd been standing up, like if she was normal and could actually feel her legs, they'd have gone all wobbly by now, and she'd be fumbling for a chair to sit on.

"My name?" Kate said. "I don't understand."

"This." Liz picked up the Thelwell pad.

Holly stared at it. She had one in purple, just like Kate's, only with her own name on it. All the team members had them. Angela's was bright yellow, Robin had blue, and Sue got a green one. The notepads were Mom's thank-you gift to the kids for winning the challenge cup.

Liz tore off a pink sticky note. "One of these," she said, waving it beneath Kate's nose, "was stuck to that empty pack of Marlboros."

Holly opened her mouth, but no sound came out.

Helplessly, she stared at Kate, willing her to say something, to prove it wasn't true. But Kate just jammed her fingers into her t-shirt pocket, turned even paler than Mom, and burst into tears.

* * *

Wiping her eyes, Kate tried to explain—her missing cell phone, the note with her father's number, and that miserable cigarette pack. Maybe, if this hadn't come on top of everything else, Liz would listen and they could work through it. But she'd tuned Kate out.

"You purposely disobeyed me."

"I know," Kate said. "And I'm sorry."

"Even if you didn't start that fire," Liz went on, "you went to the barn after I'd strictly forbidden it. I want you to pack your stuff. I'll call your aunt to tell her what's happened, and then I'll drive you to the village."

"Mom, that's crazy. You can't fire Kate. Who'll ride Buccaneer on Sunday?" Holly said.

Liz waved her off. "I will."

Kate shriveled like a spent balloon. Angela had finally won. She got what she wanted. Mrs. Dean, too. Kate would leave Timber Ridge, and right now she couldn't wait to go. Even Aunt Marion's cottage with its lumpy spare bed was better than this misery.

In less than ten minutes, Kate was packed. She dragged her suitcase and bulging knapsack into the kitchen just as Liz was picking up the phone.

"Please, don't call my aunt. I'll tell her."

Liz shrugged. "Suit yourself."

* * *

Determined not to cry, Holly sniffed and looked around her half-empty room. Well, it wasn't really half-empty. It just seemed that way, even though nothing had changed. The same ribbons and trophies filled her shelves, familiar posters covered her walls, and the Breyer horse mobile that dangled above her rumpled bed had been there forever. But without Kate, the room felt incomplete, like a big part of Holly had suddenly gone missing.

Had Kate really been smoking? In the barn?

It was beyond ridiculous. She'd never do that.

On the other hand, Kate had been acting kind of weird the past few days. She hadn't told Holly about racing Angela, nor had she apologized—well, not properly—for being snarky over Holly shaving her legs.

Holly rolled toward her bed. She wanted to fling herself on it, to wind up her feet and kick the wall. But flinging and kicking weren't part of her repertoire these days. Instead, she lowered herself awkwardly onto her pony print comforter and gazed at the ceiling. A herd of galloping horses gazed back. Mom had stuck them up there right after the accident. For many months, it was all Holly had to look at.

Kate had promised to call.

But would she?

Holly wasn't sure about anything any more.

* * *

Kate pulled on her heavy rubber work gloves. Aunt Marion grew prize-winning roses and spent countless hours in her tiny garden with pruning shears and a wheel-barrow. All she talked about were hybrid teas and flori-bundas.

First thing Saturday morning, she'd pressed Kate into service, hauling mulch and turning the compost pile. At least it was better than sitting around feeling sorry for herself.

Kate grabbed a pitchfork and tried not to fret.

Right about now, the team would be practicing the musical ride. In a final dress rehearsal, they'd be circling and wheeling and riding across the outdoor ring while trying not to bump into one another.

Had Robin managed to braid the green ribbons into Chantilly's mane without tying her fingers in knots? Would Magician stand still long enough for Sue to spray his hooves with green glitter? Was Buccaneer behaving for Liz? Did he need a double dose of Life Savers?

Five times Kate punched in Holly's cell number, and five times she cancelled the call before it went through. Holly said she'd be in touch.

But would she?

Sunday was the worst. Kate didn't want to leave her cocoon in Aunt Marion's spare bed, even though it was lumpy and full of crumbs from the cookies she'd pigged out on the night before. Finally, she got up at noon and found her aunt in the garden, deadheading roses

"Aren't you going to the party?" Marion said.

Kate yawned. "No."

"Why not?" Marion snipped off a withered bud.

"I don't feel like it."

"Oh, come along, Kate," Marion said. "Change out of those ratty pajamas, and I'll drive you to the barn." She pulled off her gloves and dropped them in a bucket of potting soil. "You look like a month's worth of wet Mondays."

"Thanks, but I'm not going."

Aunt Marion didn't know the real reason she'd left Timber Ridge. Kate just said that Liz's foot was all better and they didn't need her any more. It was a totally lame explanation that had more holes than a colander, but Aunt Marion didn't push.

Kate slouched back into her room and slammed the door. Tacked to the mirror above her bureau was the blue-and-gold ribbon she'd won on Magician at the Hampshire Classic. The team photo she'd so happily posed for was propped against her riding helmet.

It all seemed a million years ago.

* * *

The Timber Ridge maintenance crew had worked over-time. They'd erected bleachers along both sides of the outdoor ring and built a raised platform with a green canopy for dignitaries and special guests—Jennifer's parents, of course, and her Olympic grandmother, who'd flown over from England. Mrs. Dean, in a flowery hat and high heels, would shortly hold forth on the micro-phone.

Holly hitched up her long, purple skirt. It kept getting tangled in her wheels. Mom's lovely Spanish shawl was too warm, so she stuffed it behind her. Adam still hadn't shown up, and the musical ride was about to begin.

"Ladies and gentlemen, honored guests," boomed Mrs. Dean's voice. "Welcome to Timber Ridge. For your esteemed pleasure, we are proud to present our prize-winning drill team."

Holly cocked an eyebrow. *Prize-winning?*

The only prize was that pack of Life Savers Mom had awarded Kate for tumbling off Buccaneer last week. He made them all laugh by nudging her pockets with his nose like a greedy toddler while she brushed dirt off her breeches.

"They will perform a ride of exquisite loveliness," Mrs. Dean babbled on, unaware of how silly she

135

sounded, "that will leave you breathless. So please sit back and enjoy."

Holly's earphones hummed. She flicked a couple of switches on the sound board she was plugged into and cued the first CD. A remix of Lady Gaga and Michael Jackson rocked the loudspeakers.

The barn doors opened, and the Timber Ridge team trotted out. Hooves flashed and ribbons fluttered. In front, Jennifer carried five helium-filled green balloons— one for each rider. Rebel wore green tassels in his mane and a feathery plume between his ears.

Six bars into "Thriller," the riders halted. They doffed their green helmets and bowed toward the platform. Then Jennifer released her balloons and they spiraled upward into a dazzlingly blue sky filled with puffy white clouds. Applause erupted and Holly got all choked up.

Kate should've been part of this.

Left and right the riders peeled, in perfect formation. They circled and wheeled. They wove figure eights and serpentines and drew gasps of admiration when they cantered across the diagonal, missing one another by inches, the way they'd practiced.

"They're good," said a voice at Holly's shoulder.

She turned and lifted one earphone. "Oh, hi."

Adam held up his hands. "Sorry to interrupt. Keep going. You're doing a great job."

"Thanks." Holly felt herself blush.

Slowly, she faded her sound system, and the local Scots band took over. Amid a flourish of kilts and bagpipes, the riding team swept back into the barn.

"Wow," Adam said. "That was totally cool."

* * *

With Adam's help, Holly wheeled herself over to the club house, where the festivities continued. Flags flew, fireworks exploded, and kids with sticky fingers ran amok. The white-bearded DJ looked more like Dumbledore than Harry Potter.

But it wasn't the same without Kate.

"Where's Kate?" Adam said.

Holly faltered. "She had other plans."

"Oh?" Adam said. "Last I heard, she was supposed to ride Buccaneer. Mr. Ballantine was looking forward to seeing her."

He was here, somewhere in the crowd of guests. Holly caught sight of her mother, still in breeches and scuffed riding boots, chatting to Jennifer's parents and a tall man wearing faded Levis and Hollywood sunglasses—probably Mr. Ballantine .

At the buffet table, Angela whispered and giggled with Jennifer. They wore short, ruffled dresses that looked like lampshades, and Angela's hair was piled up in a mass of curls with a ringlet draped fetchingly over one ear. She kept glancing at Holly and Adam.

"Wanna dance?" he said.

Holly snorted. "How?"

"Like this."

He wheeled her onto the wooden dance floor that twinkled with fairy lights beneath a green-and-white-striped awning. Drums thumped and guitars wailed. Holly could actually feel it all the way down to her sparkly pink toenails, or maybe she was just imagining it. She lost herself in the beat as Adam rocked her wheelchair from side to side.

Angela tried to cut in.

"Go away," Adam said.

Or was Holly imagining that as well?

13

On Monday afternoon, Kate rode her bike to the village. Teens hung around doorways, looking bored and shiftless. Outside the hardware store, two old-timers argued the merits of hand-knitted wool socks versus the newfangled microfiber ones. Moms pushed kids in strollers and gossiped at the playground. Avoiding them all, Kate parked herself on a bench by the town pond.

She tossed stale bread to the ducks. Now what?

Find another job? But where? All she knew was horses, and there weren't any stables, other than Timber Ridge, that she could get to on a bicycle. She was fourteen, too young for a proper job, and she'd already applied for dishwasher jobs, but there were none to be found.

Aunt Marion said she'd pay her five dollars an hour to work in the garden, which was great. But Kate didn't want to spend the rest of her summer mowing grass and pulling weeds. Besides, Marion didn't really need her help. She was just trying to be nice. She'd also suggested Kate get a babysitting job, but Kate wasn't too good with little kids—kind of like her dad.

He still hadn't called her back.

A red-and-black truck drove past and pulled up outside the feed store. A fair-haired woman Kate vaguely recognized got out. Was that the instructor who'd given Holly her first therapeutic riding lesson? The woman saw Kate, gave a little wave, and strode into Village Feed and Grain.

Yes, that was definitely Pat Randolph—*Adam's mother*.

Kate waited, wondering if Adam would follow. Nobody else got out of the truck, so Kate strolled over and glanced inside. Two saddles and a red horse blanket filled the rear seat. A tangle of lead ropes sprawled across the front. On the dashboard lay a program of yesterday's events.

So, he really had gone to the party.

The screen door banged open, and Adam's mother

backed out of the feed store, arms wrapped around a bag of shavings. Kate helped her load it into the truck.

"Adam's down at the video arcade," his mom said.

Kate shoved her hands in both pockets.

"Go find him. He'd love to see you."

"Yeah?"

"I've got more errands to run." Mrs. Randolph checked her watch. "Remind Adam to meet me here in thirty minutes," she said, and hurried off.

* * *

Amid swirls of fog and black light, gigantic flat-screen monitors loomed at Kate from all sides. Cannons roared, race cars screeched, and 3-D robots exterminated each other with lasers and stun guns.

Edging her way past knots of kids hanging over pinball machines, Kate finally found Adam playing "Deadstorm Pirates." Skeletons with neon eyes battled a monster crab. Giant tentacles strangled a Spanish galleon and sank it, all hands aboard. She waited till Adam zapped the last bad guy, then touched his shoulder.

He jumped. "You scared me."

"Sorry." Kate stepped back.

A disco ball spun overhead and fragmented him into

a hundred tiny lights. His blond hair turned bright pink, then purple and lime green. His t-shirt glowed shockingly white.

"Let's get a soda," he said.

She shrugged. "Okay."

Now what? Kate had no idea. Why was she even here? This place was over the top. She felt out of step, like a donkey in a grand prix dressage class. Adam pushed through a rear door and into a small courtyard. In the far corner, a guy with dreadlocks sold hot dogs and popcorn. Adam bought two root beers and a carton of fries.

Kate plunked herself down at a picnic table.

He sat opposite, straddling the bench, and pushed a large plastic cup toward her. She hated root beer, but she sipped it anyway and picked up a fry.

"Why didn't you come yesterday?" he said.

The fry tasted good. Kate snagged two more and doused them with ketchup. "I had stuff to do."

"Like what?"

"Oh, you know. Just stuff."

Adam twirled his straw. "Holly missed you."

Her stomach churned. *What had Holly told him? Did he know about Kate's wild race with Angela, the stupid fire? Did he know she'd been kicked out? By now, prob-*

ably everyone knew. It didn't take long for gossip to sprint through a village the size of this one.

Adam scooped up a handful of fries. "We had a blast, and the party was great, but Holly kept checking her phone, you know, like she was hoping for a text or a call."

Kate bit her lip. *So was I.*

* * *

Holly gazed at the pool and wanted to swim. She could get in okay, but getting out was still a struggle, and there was nobody around to help. Mom had taken the younger kids to a 4-H treasure hunt with Robin and Sue. Angela and Jen had gone trail riding—not that either of them would bother to get their hands wet by hauling her out of the water.

For the tenth time, Holly checked her cell phone. Suppose it wasn't working or the signal was too weak? There were dead spots in the village. Perhaps Kate's Aunt Marion lived in one of them and that's why she didn't call.

Last night, Adam had told her to make the call.

"Just do it," he'd said, patting the swoosh logo on his black sweatshirt.

She hadn't told him anything, but he'd probably heard the rumors. One said Kate had set the fire on purpose; another claimed she stole money from the barn. Each was more outlandish than the one before.

Holly knew Kate hadn't started that fire.

So why not call her?

Was she scared Kate would hang up? Tell her to get lost?

What if she did? It wouldn't be the end of the world. Well, only a little bit. Holly reached for her phone.

* * *

After Adam left to meet his mother, Kate lingered in the courtyard. She had nothing else to do. Her life yawned open and empty, like a bucket of grain the horses had finished with long ago and abandoned. Something whinnied. Startled, she looked up. It whinnied again.

Omigod! It was her cell phone.

Kate ripped it from her pocket. "Hello?"

"Hi," Holly's voice said. "Are you okay?"

"No. Are you?"

"Not really. Can you come up, like right now?"

"What about your mom, and everything?" Kate gripped the phone so tight, her hand hurt.

144

"Nobody's here."

"Where are you?" Kate said, heart pounding.

"At the house, but I'm going to the barn."

"Should I meet you there?"

"No," Holly said. "It'll be safer at the shed. Twenty minutes, okay? No, give me thirty. I need to kiss my horse first, then I'll meet you outside Buccaneer's stall." There was a pause. "No, we'd better make it the tack room. Nobody will find us in there."

Kate hugged herself and grinned. "I'll bring Life Savers."

"Cool," Holly said and ended the call..

* * *

Holly pumped the air with her fist. Seeing Kate would be awesome. They could work things out, then figure a way to convince Mom that none of this was Kate's fault. Holly pumped the air again, and her cell phone squirted through her sweaty fingers like toothpaste from a tube. It clattered onto the stone patio. The case burst open and stuff flew out.

Appalled, Holly looked at it.

She tried to scoop it all up, but couldn't reach the battery without falling out of her chair. She'd cope with it later. Grabbing her pink hoodie from the porch railing, she tied it around her waist and headed for the barn.

Magician whinnied when he saw her trundling down the aisle with the bag of carrots she'd found in the feed room. Holly slid back his door and wheeled herself inside. He lowered his velvety nose into her lap. She hugged him and breathed in his wonderful horsey smell. One day, she'd ride him again.

After yesterday's noisy celebration, the place was eerily quiet. The other horses were outside in the big pasture, and Mom had all the ponies with her at the treasure hunt. Angela and Jen wouldn't be back for another hour, maybe longer. As long as Holly and Kate kept themselves hidden in the shed's tack room, they could hang out together till dark.

Holly checked her watch. She had fifteen minutes to reach the run-in shed before Kate arrived. It was an uphill slog and the ground was pitted with rocks and ruts.

She gave Magician another carrot and left his stall.

Outside Mom's office was a red plastic cooler, left over from the party. Holly grabbed two cans of warm seltzer. Thirstily, she drank one down and tucked the other in the leg pocket of her cargo pants, along with the last carrot.

* * *

Buccaneer was in the end stall. He couldn't be left alone in the paddock without the ponies because all he did was run the fence line, neighing and driving the other horses wild. He whickered and looked at her, no doubt hoping for candy.

"You'll get cavities," Holly said, offering him a carrot. "Eat this instead."

While he crunched it down, Holly negotiated the remaining ruts and rolled herself into the makeshift tack room. Magazines, newspapers, and crumpled soda cans lay strewn across the old couch. Hay and shavings littered the floor. Holly wadded up a bunch of baling twine and stuffed it into an empty grain sack. Somewhere in all this mess was an article about retired grand prix dressage horses being used for therapeutic riding. What wouldn't she give to ride one of those!

After pawing through all the magazines she could reach, Holly gave up. Maybe Kate would remember where it was. She'd been up here more recently than Holly. So had Angela. Her curling iron dangled from that loose socket Mom had been meaning to have fixed. She'd told the kids not to use it. Holly grabbed the iron's handle and gave the cord a sharp tug. No sense leaving it plugged in to cause trouble.

Something flashed.

Wisps of smoke curled from the broken socket. Sparks erupted like fireworks and landed on the couch. Within seconds, the newspaper she'd just been reading burst into flames.

Holly screamed.

She dropped the curling iron and reached for her cell phone, chanting the numbers. *Call nine-one-one, call nine-one-one* . . .

Then she remembered. Her phone was lying busted on the patio at home.

Now what?

Get out, and get out fast.

14

HOLLY YANKED HER WHEELS so hard, they jammed. The brakes had locked up. Where was the release lever? Her fingers fumbled and finally found it, right where it was supposed to be. Her wheels jerked free, and she backed out of the tack room twice as fast as she'd entered it. The couch began to smolder.

"*Fire!*" she yelled.

Where was Kate? She ought to be here by now. She'd have a phone and could call for help. Buccaneer's stall was at the other end of the shed, but how long before it caught fire as well?

Holly had to get him out, like right now.

Gripping her drive wheels, Holly churned toward him

like a tank. Her chair plowed over ruts, tilted around rocks, and skidded through a pile of manure. Buccaneer neighed, his eyes showing white. He was already covered with sweat.

Horses were even more terrified of fire than she was.

Holly maneuvered herself broadside against Buccaneer's door. From here she could just about reach the bolt. She released it and pulled the door sideways. Nothing. The door refused to slide. She pulled again, even harder. It didn't budge an inch.

Buccaneer's neighs grew louder. He threw himself at the heavy kick walls, then reared and banged his head on the rafters. Desperately, she looked at the tack room. Smoke poured out the open door. A gust of wind blew it in her direction.

Holly choked. She rubbed her eyes and saw another fire—a burning car, ambulances, fire trucks and hoses, and her lying on the sidewalk, helpless and unable to move.

"Help!" Holly shouted. "Help! Someone, please help!"

With both hands, she yanked at the door again, then realized what was wrong. It didn't slide. It opened outward, and her wheelchair was blocking it.

Flames burst through the tack room's roof.

Buccaneer screamed like a banshee and crashed around his stall. The building shook. Any minute now, it'd be a blazing inferno.

With a mighty lurch, Holly yanked her chair backward, out of the way. The door swung open. Buccaneer stopped crashing and cowered in the far corner.

"Come on," Holly yelled. "Move it."

He shrank even farther away.

For a frantic moment, they stared at one another—a girl who couldn't walk and a horse too terrified to move. Holly bit down hard on her fear. One of them had to do something, or they'd both go up in flames.

Holly launched herself forward and landed face down in the dirt. In a flash, she reared up on both elbows. Tears streamed down her cheeks. Stones and gravel scraped her arms as she crawled forward like a soldier on combat maneuvers. Breathing hard, she reached the door frame. Beside it was a wooden ladder, bolted to the wall, left over from the days when there was a hay loft on top of the shed.

Holly grasped the lowest rung. Its splintery wood bit into her hands. She grabbed the next rung and hauled herself upright, rung by painful rung, until she was on her wobbly feet.

Sparks landed beside her.

Buccaneer let out a bellowing neigh.

The smoke was getting thicker. It oozed through gaps in the wooden planks. Somehow, she had to get inside the stall and get him out. He wouldn't do it by himself.

Leaning against the wall, Holly whipped off her hoodie. She soaked it with seltzer from the can in her pocket and wrapped it around her neck, covering her nose and mouth. This would help keep the smoke out.

Buccaneer wore a red halter. Holly focused on that one thing and stumbled toward it. One step, then two. Arms outstretched, she grabbed his noseband with both hands and hung on.

It galvanized him into action. He barreled forward, dragging Holly with him. Out the door they went. Her legs scrambled to keep up, but they seemed to be moving on their own. One of her rubber clogs flew off, and her bare foot scraped across the gravel.

Pain shot up Holly's leg.

She released her death grip on Buccaneer's halter, curled herself into a ball, and rolled away from his flailing hooves. Her last memory before passing out was of him racing across the paddock, mane and tail flying free.

* * *

With all the strength she possessed, Kate wrapped her arms around Holly's limp body and dragged her farther from the blaze. Her empty wheelchair lay tipped on its side, in front of Buccaneer's open door. Into her cell phone, Kate barked out details for the local fire department.

"Five minutes," the dispatcher said.

Almost immediately, Kate heard the fire house siren.

Holly moaned. "Where am I?"

"It's okay," Kate said. "You're safe."

"Buc—Buccaneer?"

"He's okay, too."

Holly's pale face was smeared with soot. Scratches covered her arms and legs; her right foot was raw and bleeding. Kate pulled the wet hoodie from Holly's neck and gently wrapped it around her foot.

"Ouch," Holly said. "That hurts."

More flames erupted. Smoke billowed from the shed. There was an ear-splitting crack, and a burning timber fell across Holly's abandoned wheelchair.

"What happened?" Kate said. "The fire, how did it—?"

"My fault," Holly whimpered. "That loose socket. It blew up when I pulled Angela's curling iron out."

Kate's eyes narrowed. "Was it hot, like turned on?"

"No."

Down the driveway came Mrs. Dean in her silver Mercedes and Sue Piretti's mother in her SUV. Galloping along the paddock fence, Buccaneer neighed. Another horse answered, then Angela and Jennifer rode into view.

Jennifer flung herself off Rebel. "Holly, are you okay?"

"Yeah."

Buccaneer neighed again.

"Want me to catch him?" Jennifer said.

Kate nodded. "But you'll need these." She pulled a roll of Life Savers from her pocket. "And hurry, before the fire department gets here."

"No worries." Jennifer handed her horse's reins to Angela. "Hang onto him, okay?"

Jennifer unclipped the lead rope from around Rebel's neck and held it behind her back. Then she crunched nonchalantly on a Life Saver as she approached Buccaneer..

The sirens drew closer.

"Leave the gate open for them," Kate yelled.

Jennifer gave her a thumbs-up.

Mrs. Dean tottered toward them, high heels catching

154

on ruts and clumps of burdock. She reached for Angela's boot. "Darling, are you all right?"

"Of course, I am," Angela snapped. "But the shed isn't." She glared at Kate. "So, you started another fire, huh?"

"She wasn't even here," Holly yelled. "It was your stupid—"

"Has anyone called Liz?" Kate said.

She'd just put two and two together and come up with an alarming five. If Angela's curling iron wasn't switched on, it couldn't have started the fire. It had to be the loose socket, and that was Liz's fault for not getting it fixed.

"I called her," said Mrs. Piretti. "She's on her way."

Within minutes, firemen in big boots and yellow helmets swarmed into the field. Water gushed from giant hoses. An ambulance disgorged two medics who ran up to Holly with a stretcher.

"I'm okay, really," she insisted.

"Your foot's bleeding," the older medic said. He snapped a blood-pressure cuff on Holly's arm. "It must hurt."

"Big time," Holly said, and winced. "I'm loving it."

There was a massive rumble, like rolling thunder, and

the burning shed collapsed into itself. Mrs. Dean gave an angry gasp, then confronted the fire chief.

"You've got to find out what caused this disaster," she said.

He glowered at Kate. "Don't worry, we'll soon get our answers."

* * *

In the ambulance with Holly, Kate tried to piece it all together. She'd found Holly on the ground, half-conscious, and at least twenty feet from her overturned wheelchair.

"How did you get out of it?"

Amid tears and laughter, Holly explained what happened.

"You walked?" Kate said. "Honestly?"

"Yes, cross my heart, but don't tell Mom, okay? I want to surprise her."

"Some surprise," Kate said and punched in Liz's number. She handed Holly her cell phone. No way did she want to talk to Liz right now. Maybe she could quietly disappear before Liz showed up at the hospital.

But Holly wouldn't hear of it.

"No," she said, firmly. "It's time Mom learned the truth."

Lights flashing, the ambulance pulled up at the emergency room, and Holly was whisked inside on a gurney. Kate ran to keep up. In a curtained cubicle, a nurse removed the blood-stained pink hoodie from Holly's foot, then disappeared to find a doctor.

From outside the curtain came the sound of Liz's voice.

"Quick, Kate," Holly said. "Help me."

Before Kate had time to argue, Holly slid off the bed, leaned heavily against Kate, and took two faltering steps as her astonished mother pushed aside the cubicle curtain.

15

Liz rushed forward and wrapped her arms around Holly. "I can't believe it," she said. "Was I seeing things, or did you really just walk?"

"It was the fire, Mom," Holly said. "It unlocked my brain."

Liz hugged her daughter like she never wanted to let go. Kate felt a pang of envy. She could barely remember her own mother's arms. She died when Kate was nine.

Holly gasped. "Mom, I can't breathe."

"Sorry." Liz helped her back onto the bed.

The nurse bustled in, followed by an ER doctor in green scrubs with a stethoscope around his neck. He listened to Holly's lungs, then examined her foot and said it was nothing more serious than a few scrapes and bruises, but they'd x-ray it just to be sure.

"I can move it, see?" Holly wiggled her toes.

The doctor didn't seem impressed until Liz explained about Holly's paralysis and how this was some sort of miracle.

"No miracle," the doctor said, smiling. "Just the human mind doing amazing things we can't explain."

After cleaning up Holly's foot, the nurse wheeled her off to get it x-rayed. Liz went with them, and Kate thought seriously about slipping out the door. Aunt Marion's cottage wasn't far from the hospital. She could walk there easily. But she'd promised Holly not to bail out, so she sat down to wait.

Liz came back first. "Holly tells me I owe you a big apology."

"Not just big," Holly said, from behind her mother. She held out her arms, as far as they would stretch. "Huge and enormous, Mom. You have no idea how enormous."

"Kate, I'm sorry," Liz said. "I hope you'll forgive me."

Embarrassed, Kate looked at the floor. When grown-ups said they were sorry, it always felt awkward, like you ought to be apologizing to them, instead of the other way around.

Holly said, "But you don't know all of it, Mom. There's more."

"Can it wait till we get home?"

"You mean we can leave?" Holly said. "Like right now?"

The nurse brought her a metal walker. "Only if you promise to behave yourself."

Holly wrinkled her nose. "Those are for old people."

"And for young 'uns who need to learn how to walk again," said her mother. "So no arguments, okay?"

* * *

After Holly insisted on walking up the wheelchair ramp by herself, Kate helped Liz bundle her inside. They settled her in the wing chair with her bandaged foot on a plump cushion. Kate brought her a glass of milk and three chocolate chip cookies.

Holly rolled her eyes. "Dessert *before* dinner. I love it."

"Pizza or Chinese?" Liz brandished two take-out menus.

"Hot dogs and ice cream. With lots of mustard."

"Blech," Liz said.

Kate jumped up. "I'll fix it."

"Don't forget the pickles," Holly said.

Glad for something to do, Kate ran into the kitchen. Was it only three days ago that she'd stood in this very spot, being bawled out by Liz for stuff that wasn't her fault? It felt like three years. And, yes, they could explain all the trouble Angela had caused, but that broken socket in the shed was Liz's responsibility.

Kate pulled a package of hot dogs from the freezer. She wouldn't want to be in Liz's shoes when the fire chief called with the results of his investigation.

* * *

With two fingers, Holly scooped up the last of her butter-crunch ice cream. Nothing had ever tasted so good—not even the meringue cherry torte she'd shared with Adam at the party.

He'd texted Kate to make sure everyone was okay.

News got around this place so fast that it made Holly's head spin. On Facebook and Twitter, Angela was already blaming Kate for the fire—not by name, but with innuendo and sly hints that were big enough to trip over.

Holly took a deep breath. "Mom, listen to me."

"Okay," Liz said. "Shoot."

"Remember all the stupid stuff that's been happening?"

"I hate to say this, but remind me."

"The lesson mix-up, that note you never got about Jennifer's horse, the ruined photo," Holly said.

Her mother frowned. "What about them?"

"None of it was Kate's fault."

"But Kate said—"

"She was covering up."

"Who for?" Liz said.

Holly played her trump card. "Angela."

"That's ridiculous," Liz said. "Why would Kate do that?"

"To stop you from yelling at Mrs. Dean."

"I don't get it," Liz said. "Is there something I'm missing here?"

"Kate was afraid you'd lose your job if you told Mrs. Dean what Angela was up to," Holly said, as patiently as she could. Mom always acted dumb whenever this subject reared its ugly head. "That's why we didn't say anything."

Liz sighed. "Haven't we been through this before?"

"Yes, but—"

"Look, I appreciate the help, but from now on," Liz said, "I want you kids to promise you'll tell me when things go wrong. If I'm going to cope with Mrs. Dean, honestly and openly, I need to know what's happening, okay? You can't take it on your own shoulders to try and fix things. Life doesn't work that way."

Holly glanced at Kate. "We didn't know what else to do."

There was a lengthy pause. Then Liz said, "I thought all this nonsense was over when Angela got her gold medal at the Hampshire Classic."

"Get real, Mom," Holly said. "Angela's jealous of Kate, and she's steaming mad over not being allowed to ride Buccaneer."

"She's not competent enough."

Holly snorted. "We know, but try telling her that."

Liz's cell phone rang. She answered and got up to pace the kitchen floor. Holly could hardly wait to be able to do that again herself. She looked down at her feet and wiggled them to make sure she hadn't dreamed all this.

"Yes, yes, she's fine," Liz said. "And thank you. Yes, I'll tell her." There was a long pause, and Liz's expression changed from puzzled to a cautious smile. Holly tried to guess what was going on and was completely baffled when her mom said, "It's okay with me as long as you clear it with Mrs. Dean." Still smiling, she slipped the phone back into her pocket.

"What?" Holly almost screamed. "Who was that?"

"Giles Ballantine."

"He's asked you on a date?" Holly said. "But why would he have to clear it with Mrs. Dean first?"

She winked at Kate, and they both started to giggle.

Liz gave a snort of exasperation. "He wanted to make sure you were okay, and—"

"What about Buccaneer?" Kate said. "He's not leaving is he?"

"Not yet, so stop worrying," Liz said.

The front doorbell rang.

"I'll get it." Kate leaped to her feet and raced from the kitchen. Moments later, she was back with an armload of white roses. Two dozen at least, and all with long stems.

"I knew it," Holly said. "Mom, he *did* ask you out."

"These are you for you," Kate said, turning to Holly.

"Me?" Holly stared at the roses. She'd never been given flowers before. "Who're they from?"

"Read the card," said her mother.

Holly opened it. *My humble thanks to a brave young woman for saving my horse—GB*

"Cool," Kate said.

Holly sniffed her roses. "Yeah."

"There's more," Liz said. She got up to find a vase. "Mr. Ballantine's film company wants to use Timber Ridge for a location shot in their next film."

"Now that's *really* cool," Holly said. "I'll get to be a star."

* * *

For two days, she got her wish. Everyone, it seemed to Kate, stopped by the barn to see Holly, except Angela who was still posting lies on the web.

"You were *so* brave," said Robin.

Sue hugged her. "I couldn't have done what you did."

U R ORSUM, Adam texted.

Even Holly had trouble figuring that one out.

The maintenance crew got busy hauling away the wreckage, but still the fire chief hadn't called. Kate began to worry. She and Holly had talked about the broken plug and agreed that Angela's curling iron probably wasn't to blame. So where did that leave Liz? She knew the electrical box was a hazard, but had she called anyone to fix it?

They were in Liz's office, eating lunch, when the barn

phone rang. Liz answered, listened for a moment, then hung up. Her face was unreadable, like she'd just received more news but couldn't tell if it was good or bad.

"Mom, what it is?" Holly put down her sandwich.

"That was the fire chief."

"What did he say?"

"Faulty wiring," Liz said.

Kate's heart did a double whump. Liz could lose her job over this. Besides the old shed, quite a few saddles and bridles had gone up in flames, too. "Was it that socket in the tack room?"

"Yes, but Mrs. Dean's not going to like it."

"Why?" Holly said.

"Because she canceled my work order to get that plug fixed," Liz said. "She said it wasn't worth it. The shed would soon be torn apart and turned into a clubhouse."

Holly's smile lit up the room. "Yes!"

Kate gave her a high five. Liz was off the hook. This whole mess was Mrs. Dean's fault, and it was in writing. Surely the homeowners' association wouldn't let her wriggle out of this one.

16

HOLLY PRACTICED WALKING in the aisle. She said having an audience of horses inspired her. She fell often—sprawling like a rag doll amid hay bales and shavings—but was protected by leather gloves and knee pads, and Kate was always there to pick her up. Finally, after three days of intense effort, Holly managed to walk from one end of the barn to the other without crashing to the ground.

Liz said, "I think you're ready."

"What for?"

"Magician."

"Yikes!" Holly lost her balance and promptly fell over.

Feeling warm and fuzzy inside, Kate led Magician

from his stall. This was beyond amazing. They'd not expected Holly to be ready for action so soon. But when Liz saw her doing so well, she'd told Kate to tack him up. Holly hadn't noticed. She'd been too busy bossing her legs around.

In the arena, Magician stood like a marble statue beside the mounting block. He didn't move a muscle, even when Holly's foot dug into his side as she clambered on board. Her smile radiated sunshine.

"How does it feel?" Liz said.

"Unbelievable!" Holly's smile grew wider. "This is awesome, Mom. I can feel him, even through my boots." She eyed the cross-rails.

"No," Liz said. "Don't even think about it."

"Next week." Holly grinned and gathered up her reins. Then, with Liz walking proudly beside her, she rode her own horse for the first time in two years.

Watching them brought a lump to Kate's throat. No wonder Holly had won all those ribbons and trophies. With her natural seat and quiet hands, she looked as if she'd been born in the saddle.

"Brilliant, yes?" Jennifer seemed to appear out of nowhere.

Kate glanced uneasily toward the door. "Where's Angela?"

"Around, I guess."

Something about Jennifer had changed. It wasn't just her clothes or her accent, but the way she was looking at Kate with a friendly grin, like she had that day in the barn when they'd groomed Skywalker together. Still, she was part of Angela's crowd, and she'd believed all the venom Angela had spewed.

Unsure what to think, Kate shifted a few feet away. She hadn't seen either of them since the fire, when Jennifer had taken care of Buccaneer. But that was probably because Holly was hurt and people were watching.

"I told Angela to stop," Jennifer said.

"Stop what?"

"Saying stuff that's not true. Nobody believes her."

Kate tore her eyes away from Holly, now jogging in small circles on a lunge line, and stared at Jennifer. "They don't?"

"Nah, she's lost half her friends on Facebook, including me."

"You mean—?"

"Yeah, and I'm sorry for being a jerk to you."

While Kate was absorbing this, Jennifer surprised her again. "My grandmother owns Beaumont Park."

If this had come from Angela, Kate would've dismissed it as another tall tale. But Jennifer's grandmother

169

was a famous rider, and Beaumont Park was one of the best equestrian centers in England.

"For real?" Kate said.

Jennifer grinned. "My gran's a pistol." She pulled a crumpled brochure from her pocket. "This is her new program, for young riders. Take a look."

It was heady stuff.

Kate gazed at photos of horses with glossy coats, gleaming tack, and white saddle pads that bore the flags of different countries. Well-known names jumped off the page—Will Hunter, Nicole Hoffman, and Ineke Van Klees, the Dutch rider who'd won Olympic gold at nineteen. They'd all trained at Beaumont Park.

Kate sighed. "I'd love to go there."

"You can," Jennifer said. "I'm going next summer, and Gran's invited you to come with me."

"You're kidding."

"Nope."

"But why me?"

"Because I told her how good you are."

Kate leaned heavily against the rail. Her father could never pay for this. His expeditions were only partly funded by his university. He coughed up the rest from lecture fees and writing books that only appealed to people like him who were nutty enough to chase butterflies through impenetrable jungles.

"Thanks," Kate mumbled, "but my dad couldn't afford it."

"No worries," Jennifer said. "It's on the house, a kind of working scholarship. You'd only have to pay for air fare." She nodded toward Holly. "I'll get Gran to invite her, too."

"Wow," Kate said, suddenly tongue-tied.

* * *

Ten minutes later, Jennifer helped Holly unsaddle Magician and told her about Beaumont Park's new training program. "There are three dressage rings, two indoor arenas, more jumps than you've ever seen before, and a cross-country course that's bigger than Badminton." Her eyes shone with fun. "It'll be a blast, and you've got to come."

"Sounds awesome," Holly said, "but what about Angela?"

"She wasn't invited," Jennifer replied.

"Seriously?"

"Yup. Gran doesn't like her."

Holly shot a triumphant look at Kate. This was perfect. In fact, it was better than perfect. Even if they'd brainstormed till infinity, they couldn't have dreamed up a better way for Kate to get her own back on Angela Dean.

Don't miss **Book 3** in the exciting
Timber Ridge Riders series.

Riding for the Stars

A movie is being filmed at Timber Ridge
Stables and one lucky girl is actually going
to be in it. Of course, Angela Dean wants
the part, but Kate McGregor wants it even
more. With money from the movie, Kate can
make her special dream come true—she can
buy a horse of her own.

What will Angela do to stop her?

She's tried all kinds of dirty tricks in the
past . . . but now a beloved horse is missing.

Would Angela go that far?

Win the next book

Riding for the Stars

Book Three of Timber Ridge Riders

Send me an email to:
TimberRidgeRiders@gmail.com
Put Racing into Trouble in the subject line, and I'll
enter your name into a drawing for a free copy of
Riding for the Stars

For more information about the series, visit my web site:

www.maggiedana.com

About the Author

MAGGIE DANA'S FIRST RIDING LESSON, at the age of five, was less than wonderful. She hated it so much, she didn't try again for another three years. But all it took was the right horse and the right instructor and she was hooked.

After that, Maggie begged for her own pony and was lucky enough to get one. Smoky was a black New Forest pony who loved to eat vanilla pudding and drink tea, and he became her constant companion. Maggie even rode him to school one day and tethered him to the bicycle rack ... but not for long because all the other kids wanted pony rides, much to their teachers' dismay.

Maggie and Smoky competed in Pony Club trials and won several ribbons. But mostly, they had fun—trail riding and hanging out with other horse-crazy girls. At horse camp, Maggie and her teammates spent one night sleeping in the barn, except they didn't get much sleep because the horses snored. The next morning, everyone was tired and cranky, especially when told to jump without stirrups.

Born and raised in England, Maggie now makes her home on the Connecticut shoreline. When not mucking stalls or grooming shaggy ponies, Maggie enjoys spending time with her family and writing the next book in her TIMBER RIDGE RIDERS series.

47392672R00110

Made in the USA
Lexington, KY
05 December 2015